SECRET PIZZA

A MIDWESTERN FAIRYTALE

BRENDAN GREELEY

Here's to good pizza!

Publisher: Party Cut Press

Editor: Mike Leonard

Copy Editor: Bridget Wrobel

DEDICATION

For my friend Rich
For my friend Jeff
For my cousin Pat, who organized the gatherings

This book is also dedicated to Casciani's Pizzeria on Joliet Road and Ledo's Pizza on La Grange Road, two legendary parlors of my youth.

CONTENTS

1

RISING CRUST

Everyone called me "Crust," but it had nothing to do with my love of pizza. Crust was a derivation of my family name, Crzytok.

I required a nickname because my given name, Carroll, left much to be desired. My dad named me after his favorite actor, Carroll O'Connor, who played lovable grump Archie Bunker on *All in the Family*. Heck, I would've preferred Archie if Dad insisted on honoring the TV show, but suppose I was lucky he didn't name me after Archie's son-in-law, Meathead. Either way, Carroll was far too serious a name. A grade school chum shortened Crzytok to Crust, and it stuck. Even teachers called me Crust.

My pastimes were TV, drawing, and baseball. I inherited my father's love of situation comedies. When I stayed home sick during the school year, I watched daytime reruns with my dad. He worked all hours for a Chicago bread manufacturer, meaning we didn't always get to catch primetime shows together.

I wasn't home alone when my dad was on the job. My grandfather lived with us. "Gloam-pa" was his nickname, given to him by me when I first learned to talk. I don't remember mispronouncing "Grandpa" in my baby talk any more than I remember my mother's face. She changed her mind about being a mom during the first year, and there were no pictures of her hanging around the house. Instead of correcting my infant mistake, Gloam-pa embraced the mispronunciation and even encouraged its use. It reminded him of the most glorious day of his youth: when Cubs catcher Gabby Hartnett connected on the "Homer in the Gloamin'" versus the Pirates at Wrigley Field as the sun set.

Hartnett's home run propelled Chicago into first place and on to clinch the National League pennant. Gloam-pa repeated the story whenever we watched an extra-inning game on WGN-TV, and daylight began to fade. I found a picture of Gabby Hartnett in my baseball almanac. Gabby had smile dimples like Gloam-pa and me, although Gloam-pa's dimples stayed hidden behind his beard. Gloam-pa's facial hair was thick and white by the time I entered the world.

Gloam-pa had a routine. He woke up before dawn and made himself two soft-boiled eggs. Six mornings per week he swam at the YMCA. Gloam-pa returned home from the Y in time to cook breakfast for Dad and me. Gloam-pa's morning kitchen smelled of pancakes and pool water. My dad believed the primary purpose of Gloam-pa's fitness routine was to suppress any resemblance to Santa Claus. "Your grandfather would rather be a wiry prune than shave his bushy beard each December."

Gloam-pa's closest friend was fellow Chicago Fire Department retiree Danny "Whiskers" Neville. Back in 1946, strapping young Danny Neville responded to a fire at a Jefferson Park three-flat. A wall collapsed during the rescue effort, but Danny was shielded from falling bricks by a sturdy cast iron stove. Danny had taken a knee next to the stove in order to coax a frightened house cat named Whiskers out from behind the appliance. He eventually succeeded in grabbing the cat and carrying it to safety. A *Chicago Sun* shutterbug snapped a photograph of the firefighter comforting the trembling kitty. The intended caption, "Whiskers the Cat and the Hero," was misprinted in the morning edition of the publication:

```
Whiskers and the Hero Cat
```

Danny's firehouse brethren plastered the walls with clippings of the miscaptioned photo. That's how Danny Neville became Whiskers. Whiskers kept tabs on the cat, who ended up living another sixteen years after the fire.

Whiskers often joined us at the house for lunch or dinner. He always arrived with a rollicking anecdote, some of which lasted the entirety of the meal. The long stories were enjoyable for me because Whiskers was naturally funny. They were fine with my father, too, as he was often short on conversational energy as he approached his next round of abbreviated sleep. Gloam-pa boasted one of the all-time great, thunderous laughs, which he unleashed throughout a Whiskers' knee-slapper. Whiskers had the thickest Chicago accent. He said "cahr" instead of "car" and "ding" instead of "thing." To be fair, the Crzytok family had a touch of the local accent too. But compared to Whiskers, we sounded like English teachers or TV news anchors. Gloam-pa missed the camaraderie of his active duty days. Whiskers' visits helped fill the void.

Gloam-pa's corned beef earned a badge of approval from Whiskers, who was supremely Irish. Gloam-pa's first battalion chief taught him how to season beef. It was also thanks to a fellow firefighter that Gloam-pa unlocked the secrets of Sauerbraten. A captain from the Portage Park neighborhood helped Gloam-pa perfect his pierogis. A bunkmate from Bucktown schooled Gloam-pa on authentic Puerto Rican paella. Gloam-pa excelled at nearly every cuisine. He had a knack for mastering recipes and adding his own twists. The one thing he refused to make on his own was pizza. That, he decided, was left to the professionals of the craft with proper pizza ovens.

Every Friday evening, Gloam-pa, Dad, and I walked over to our local pizzeria on Western Avenue. I looked forward to Pizza Friday all week long. Sometimes I'd get caught daydreaming about pizza when I was supposed to be paying attention to fractions. Dad didn't have to work on Saturdays, so he was noticeably good-natured and chipper on Pizza Fridays. Gloam-pa and my dad ordered mugs of beer, and I was permitted to guzzle as much RC Cola as I could consume. Pop on ice at a restaurant always tasted extra good.

During the week, I was allowed one pop per day from the fridge. My dad was strict about it because he didn't want my teeth to get any expensive cavities. He counted the Cokes when he got home from work to ensure I wasn't sneaking pops. Gloam-pa softly enforced my dad's rule but allowed ample wiggle room. At Wrigley Field, for instance, he'd buy me a Pepsi from the roving vendor in the first inning and an additional Pepsi around the fifth. My middle school obsession with Mountain Dew baffled Gloam-pa.

"Unnaturally bright yellow," he grimaced. "Like a Chernobyl byproduct." He'd still fork over the money to the White Hen clerk and allow me my Dew. I pressured Gloam-pa to try a sip of the nuclear beverage. He refused.

"I'll stick to ginger ale."

I drew a picture of Gloam-pa holding his gold ginger ale next to me with my yellow Mountain Dew. Gloam-pa joked that he was going to hand the drawing over to The Art Institute. If they refused to frame it for display, Gloam-pa claimed he would glue it to a gallery wall himself. I'm not sure where I got my talent for drawing. My dad was no artist and neither was Gloam-pa.

After we filled up on pizza squares each week, the three Crzytok men went home to watch Friday night television. ABC-TV featured a block of family-friendly programs. Gloam-pa and I got a kick out of the unpredictable Balki Bartokomous, a character from the show *Perfect Strangers*. My dad praised *Full House* comedian Joey Gladstone. All three of us were bowled over by the hilarious antics of TV nerd Steve Urkel on *Family Matters*. Gloam-pa spoke of Urkel as if he were a cherished member of our family.

Ahead of Christmas in 1992, Cubs general manager Larry Himes decided to let Greg Maddux, the best pitcher in baseball, leave for Atlanta in free agency. Gloam-pa found me in my room throwing a fit.

"How come Larry Himes gets to make this decision that affects all of us?" I complained. "Shouldn't fans get a vote?"

"Players come, players go. Nature of the business," Gloam-pa explained.

Business. Whenever I read that word in the Sports section, it meant something lousy was happening and fans had to swallow the consequences.

"Maddux wanted to stay in Chicago," I sulked. "He liked it here."

"Life goes on. You've still got Ryne Sandberg," Gloam-pa said.

"And Mark Grace," I added.

"Amazing Grace!" Gloam-pa emphasized. "Plenty to cheer for. Cubs will be OK."

He walked out and returned holding my winter coat.

"C'mon, let's get an ice cream cone," Gloam-pa encouraged.

"But it's winter," I objected.

"Not inside the store it isn't," Gloam-pa said. "Fine, you stay here. Gloam-pa is getting himself an ice cream cone."

I took the bait and grabbed my coat. Two scoops of peanut butter and chocolate melted away my Cubbie blues.

"Who knows, perhaps the pitcher they signed will be just as good as Maddux," Gloam-pa said, as he spooned his mocha chip ice cream.

"Jose Guzman," I filled in the player's name. "He went 16-11 for the Rangers last season."

The following spring, Major League Baseball scheduled the defending National League Champion Atlanta Braves to open the season in Chicago versus the Cubs. Atlanta's new ace, Greg Maddux, tossed a 1-0 shutout against his former team on Opening Day. When I got home from school, Gloam-pa poured me a Coke over ice and sat me down for the unhappy recap. The next day, new Cubs hurler Jose Guzman faced off against John Smoltz. Guzman took a perfect game into the eighth inning, before issuing a walk to Terry Pendleton. He kept the no-hitter going through twenty-six outs until Otis Nixon ruined it with a solid single. Gloam-pa captured the tension of each at-bat in his after-school recap. He reenacted Harry Caray's emotional play-by-play call for my amusement.

Despite his triumphant debut, Jose Guzman proved to be no Greg Maddux; impossible cleats to fill. But Gloam-pa was right about life going on. Seeing Maddux win games for another organization stunk, but it didn't dampen my Cubs fandom one iota.

Every Easter, Gloam-pa hid two plastic eggs for me to seek. Each egg contained a ticket for a future Cubs game, one for me and one for Gloam-pa. I quibbled with the need for two eggs because both tickets could easily fit in the same egg. Gloam-pa blamed the Easter Bunny for the two-egg policy.

"Why is it my job to find *your* egg?" I griped.

"Easter Bunny says I'm too old to crawl around looking for eggs, Carroll. Luckily, I have a grandson to help me out."

I also didn't appreciate the Easter Bunny rolling the tickets up so they'd fit inside the eggs. I flattened the tickets and preserved them in my sock drawer until the July or August date of the scheduled game.

I traded baseball cards with neighborhood kids in Dale Gorman's garage every other Saturday. Summer after my freshman year at Lane Tech High School, I was negotiating with some sucker in an attempt to relieve him of his Ken Griffey Jr. rookie card, when Dale showed off what he stashed behind the Christmas decorations.

"Swiped a tin of chewing tobacco," Dale said. "From the gas station."

He shoved a wad of the stuff in between his lip and gums. Then he handed me the tin.

"Just like ballplayers chew," Dale nodded. "It's awesome. You get a body buzz."

Baseball players swore by the stuff, so I figured I could give it a shot. I took a small pinch and wedged it inside my cheek. I felt pretty cool, spitting out brown saliva into a plastic cup. Then the body buzz hit, only it wasn't as awesome as Dale predicted. I was too dizzy to continue bartering for rookie cards. I got some fresh air out in the alley. That was where I puked. Must've swallowed as much of the juice as I spit out. I remember Dale's mom freaking out and calling my dad, who came and got me. He was mad. I was grounded for two weeks. Once my stomach recovered, I accepted the punishment without argument because I knew Gloam-pa was unlikely to enforce it. The Pittsburgh Pirates were coming to town to play the Cubs, and the Easter Bunny had provided us with Thursday bleacher tickets. I knew Gloam-pa didn't want to miss interacting with Pittsburgh centerfielder Andy Van Slyke, who frequently engaged in playful back-and-forth with fans. Gloam-pa and I had a soft spot for Van Slyke, despite how loudly we heckled him.

Thursday morning, I was so confident we were heading to the game that I put on my lucky "Late Night at Wrigley Field" T-shirt, purchased for me by Gloam-pa outside of Wrigley the year lights were installed for night games. The boys' large shirt was too big for me in 1988. By 1993, it was a tight squeeze.

"Might be time for a new shirt," Gloam-pa said.

"Great! We'll shop outside the ballpark today. There's one that says 'Bleacher Bum.'"

"Carroll, no ballgame today. You're still grounded."

"C'mon," I pleaded. "Dad will never find out."

"It's not about your dad finding out," Gloam-pa said. "It's for your own good. You can watch the game on TV. I have an afternoon appointment with a city pension agent."

I stomped around the kitchen and poured an enormous bowl of Froot Loops to take back to my room. I didn't come out, even at one-twenty for the game.

Pizza Friday rolled around. Dad and Gloam-pa waited by the front door.

"While we're young, Carroll," Gloam-pa bellowed.

I emerged from my room with my sketch pad in hand. I plopped onto the couch in the front room.

"You're not coming?" my dad asked.

"I'm grounded," I huffed.

Gloam-pa and my dad stood still.

"We'll bring home leftovers," Gloam-pa finally said.

I turned on the Cubs pregame show.

My dad startled me awake hours later. Sportscaster Dan Roan was recapping the Cubs game. My sketch pad sat unmarked.

"Put on a shirt," Dad said.

We paced around the Methodist Hospital waiting room until the doctor found us. Gloam-pa's heart couldn't be restarted.

The wake felt unnatural, and the funeral was the saddest day of my life. Guilt followed me everywhere.

Why did I act like such a brat on Gloam-pa's last ever Pizza Friday?

My dad went back to work. I stayed home and watched Cubs games alone. I decided Gloam-pa could still see the games from Heaven. Woody Boyd made me chuckle at a *Cheers* rerun, but then I felt even more guilty for laughing so soon after Gloam-pa died.

My dad wanted to try Pizza Friday, just the two of us. I talked him out of it. I couldn't go to the place where Gloam-pa keeled over when I wasn't there to help him.

I surely would have noticed a sign of distress. I could've done something. If only I hadn't been so stubborn.

There would be no more Pizza Fridays or homemade dinners. Without Gloam-pa's kitchen skills, we were helpless. Frozen food filled our stomachs.

For Thanksgiving, we traveled to my Great Aunt Mildred's house in Hazel Park, Michigan. Mildred was Gloam-pa's sister, and she insisted we spend the holiday at her home. A distant cousin tried to serve me stuffing, but Mildred stopped her.

"Carroll doesn't eat stuffing," Mildred said.

"Who doesn't like stuffing?" the cousin second-guessed.

My dad made me carry dishes to the sink after dinner, and I asked Mildred how she knew about my distaste for stuffing.

"Walter's letters," she said.

Walter was Gloam-pa's real name.

"He detailed practically every moment he spent with his grandson," Mildred smiled. "Said you were a gifted storyteller."

"Me?"

"You reminded him of his dear friend Whiskers with your inflection and outlook on the world."

It was a serious compliment. I blushed at the comparison to a world-class anecdote slinger like Whiskers.

Whiskers hadn't been in attendance at the services for Gloam-pa. I figured he'd been off on one of his famous voyages to his home country, where he hoisted countless pints at Irish pubs.

About a year after Gloam-pa passed, Whiskers dropped by the house to give me a gold-plated compass. His voice was hoarse and weary.

"Dis belonged ta Walter," Whiskers said. "His lucky charm back when he was on da job. Some sorta heirloom. Walter as'd me ta keep it in my safe duh-posit box."

With that, Whiskers put on his hat and turned to leave.

"Whiskers, wait," I shouted after him. "Want to join us for pizza?"

My dad was surprised. I figured the compass was a sign from Gloam-pa to stop mourning.

"Shall we walk down the block to our usual spot?" my dad asked.

I shook my head. I wasn't ready to return to our local pizzeria quite yet.

"Le's do tha ol' spot near da firehouse," Whiskers proposed. "Yur granfodder swore by da joint."

Contadino's Pizza was an eyesore. A faded, paint-chipped pasta mural on the alley side offered the only clue that the brick hovel was any sort of restaurant. Whiskers pried open the swollen front door. Indoors, the place was clean but ancient. The vinyl on our booth was worn thin. The table was uneven and marked with doodles and initials. A gray old man barged out through the floppy kitchen door. He shuffled over to our table.

"Mr. Contadino. It's me, Whiskers."

Mr. Contadino's face lit up.

"Mr. Whiskers! This guy used to be here three times a week."

"Back when I c'd eat a whole large pie by myself," Whiskers patted his gut.

"You back at the firehouse?" Mr. Contadino asked. "Whiskers—the funny guy!"

"Nah, still retired," Whiskers responded.

"Mr. Contadino, my name is Dennis Crzytok," my dad re-introduced himself. "I used to come here all the time with my father, Walter."

"I remember! Your father, I was so sorry to hear of his passing. My condolences."

My dad bowed his head in acceptance. Whiskers put his arm around me.

"An' dis is Walter's gran'son Carroll."

"Nice to meet you, young man," Mr. Contadino smiled. "Your grandfather was a faithful customer."

Mr. Contadino shouted for Mrs. Contadino to come from the kitchen and make my acquaintance. She was the same height and equally as gray as her husband. She also gushed about Gloam-pa.

I downed an RC with my antipasto but was careful not to fill up on bread. The pizza arrived, and it changed my perception of Contadino's. This was the Greg Maddux of pizzas. I bit into my first square and immediately understood why customers felt the need to carve their names in the booth. I no longer noticed the sticky floor, the dingy light fixtures, or the broken jukebox. I reached a new level of pizza consciousness.

Whiskers took me to a Cubs game not long after our pizza outing. San Diego was in town, and the Padres' Tony Gwynn was chasing a .400 batting average. It would be my first and last game of 1994, as a strike abruptly ended the baseball season a few days later. Gwynn collected three hits to raise his average to .392. I refused to give Gwynn much credit, conserving my applause for hometown shortstop Shawon Dunston's pursuit of a significantly less historic .300 batting average. The famous Wrigley Field "Shawon-O-Meter" dropped to .286 that day, as Dunston went hitless. Whiskers was impressed by my strict allegiance.

"Yur loyal ta yur Cubs. I'll gi' you dat. Yur grampa was da same."

Whiskers had free parking at the firehouse on Waveland across from the ballpark. He let me drive his old Lincoln, as I was newly licensed and eager to get behind the wheel. As I turned left onto Irving Park Road, Whiskers launched into a confession.

"Da las' Cubs game yur granfodder was s'posed ta take you to, he missed it cuz uh me. And I'm real sorry 'bout dat, kid."

Whiskers turned down the volume on the postgame radio show.

"Dere was a game 'gainst da Pirates, but Walter had ta bring me ta da doctor. Dey were doin' tests. I wuddn't permitted ta drive myself. He insisted on takin' me."

"What kind of tests?"

"My t'roat and limp nodes. Dere was cancer in dere."

Whiskers paused before reassuring me.

"Bedder now, dey removed da tumor."

"That's good."

"Don' ever chew tobacco, kid. Ain't worth it. Trus' me."

Gobsmacked by Whiskers' words, I blew a red light and nearly hit a pedestrian.

"Holy cow, junior! T'ought you aced yur drivin' exam!"

Whiskers scrutinized my driving until I dropped myself off and left him to slide behind the wheel for his own journey home. I went to my bedroom and fell face first on the bed. I sobbed—*really* sobbed. Whiskers had unwittingly dropped a puzzle piece in my lap. Gloam-pa witnessed the long term effects of Whiskers' vice and didn't want me heading down tobacco road. That was why he enforced the punishment—to make the lesson stick. The burst of tears released remorse and fatigue I'd carried around for a year. I slept.

I woke up with the sun and felt inspired. I snuck to the kitchen and found Gloam-pa's mixing bowl. I'd watched Gloam-pa's routine many times, and the steps were simple. My dad wandered out, half-asleep.

"Pancakes?" he asked.

"It's been awhile," I said.

"Sure has," Dad nodded. "Miss the smell of pancakes in the house."

My dad poured the orange juice. We ate breakfast together. He left for work that afternoon, and I used my alone time to dig through Gloam-pa's recipes. I walked to the Jewel and bought ingredients for Gloam-pa's meatloaf. I waited until late night to start cooking so the meatloaf would be fresh out of the oven when my dad got home.

"Making dinner, son? Atta boy!"

Dad's enthusiasm waned, as did my newfound kitchen pride, when I tried to cut a slice of meatloaf out of the pan. It was goopy in the middle and burnt on the outside. My dad made the best of it. He covered his plate in ketchup and acted like it was a decent dinner.

"You don't have to pretend," I said. "Meatloaf catastrophe. Not sure what I did wrong."

"Not bad for your first try," Dad said. "Better than I could do."

The next day I slept until noon and bummed around. I wasn't depressed or anything, just lazy. The rest of the week was pretty much the same. I'd wake up at noon, eat an enormous bowl of cereal, and watch TV all day.

At the end of the week, my dad came home and handed me an envelope. Inside was a United Airlines ticket to Detroit.

"Your Great Aunt will pick you up at the airport," Dad instructed.

"A week with Mildred? Sounds boring."

"Son, nothing could be more dull than your current daily routine."

He had a point. The next morning, I took the CTA Blue Line train to O'Hare for my flight. Aunt Mildred was there waiting when I landed in Detroit. After showing me my accommodations, Mildred took me to Hazel Park Raceway. I didn't know much about horses, but harness racing sure was a blast, especially with Mildred seeking my advice at the wagering window. One of my picks was a winner. Mildred said it was enough to earn me a Coney dog and a milkshake.

Mildred wanted my stay to be culturally enriching. On day two, she took me to the Great Lakes Museum and the Motown Museum. The exhibits were cool, particularly the scale model ships and the "My Girl" stuff. The latter reminded me of the time we watched the Macaulay Culkin/Anna Chlumsky movie named after the song, and Gloam-pa handed me his handkerchief, but I pretended I wasn't crying, and Gloam-pa pretended to believe me. Mildred bought me a Stevie Wonder T-shirt at the gift shop. I asked if we could have Coney dogs and milkshakes again for lunch. Mildred knew a place downtown.

"Get your fill now," she warned. "Tonight we're eating home-cooked food."

Back at Great Aunt Mildred's house, I aimed straight for the couch and flipped on the television. Great Aunt Mildred stood in front of the TV. I craned my neck to see around her.

"You're needed in the kitchen," Great Aunt Mildred said. "You're my sous chef."

"What's a sous chef?"

"An assistant. To help with dinner."

"We just ate. Besides, I'm no good in the kitchen. Trust me. I made a meatloaf so bad even the alley rats ignored it."

Great Aunt Mildred countered my arguments with ease.

"First, dinner takes time to prepare, and another appetite will arrive in due time. Second, failure in the kitchen is part of the process. Do you think Julia

Child succeeded the first time she tried making a casserole? Try. Fail. Try again. Fail again. The most important thing is to keep trying. Only then will you find success."

Next thing I knew, I was wearing an apron and peeling potatoes in Mildred's kitchen. She spread out all the ingredients for her beef stew and directed me to add each to the pot at the appropriate time. Great Aunt Mildred taught me how to thicken the broth with cornstarch. The aroma of beef stew filled the air and built up the impending appetite Mildred had foreseen. When the stew was finally ready, she filled two bowls.

"Rewarding, isn't it?" Great Aunt Mildred asked. "You made this delicious meal."

It was tasty.

Great Aunt Mildred taught me one recipe per day for the rest of my week in Michigan:

- Monday: Beef Stir-Fry

- Tuesday: Pork Tenderloin

- Wednesday: Chili

- Thursday: BBQ chicken thighs

- Friday: Pan-fried lake perch

Saturday we stopped for Coney dogs and a milkshake on the way to Detroit Metro Airport. I examined the dogs to consider the preparation that went into the culinary delight.

Upon my return home, I claimed Gloam-pa's collection of utensils, pots, and measuring cups. There were three cookbooks in his kitchen. I chose the most stained book with the flimsiest spine. In the weeks leading up to Labor Day, I hardly left the kitchen, not even for reruns of *The Simpsons*. "The Great Aunt Mildred Visit" worked just like my dad hoped, and he reaped the benefit with hot meals each night. Dad applauded my culinary growth, while I pleaded with him to be honest about what he liked and disliked. With some prodding, he'd admit "this could use less garlic" and that "is a bit chewy." I took notes and watched TV chefs to improve my techniques.

On Thanksgiving, instead of turkey, I made Gloam-pa's corned beef. We invited Whiskers to celebrate with us.

"Beef is real nize an' tender," Whiskers said. "Pass da mashed, wouldya?"

"You oughta consider culinary school, Carroll," my dad suggested.

"Dat wha chu wanna do?" Whiskers asked. "Be a chef?"

I shrugged. I hadn't really thought about being anything.

"You know of any restaurants that might need a hand in the kitchen?" Dad asked Whiskers.

"Couldn't hurt ta ask around," Whiskers nodded.

"You mean like a job?" I asked.

One minute Whiskers is complimenting my corned beef, and the next minute my dad is pushing him to get me hired.

"It's time, Carroll," my dad sighed. "Don't get me wrong, I'm happy to buy you new kitchen appliances. But it's gotten out of control. Half of my last paycheck went to Ron Popiel."

It was true. I was addicted to ordering countertop devices from Ron Popiel, Jack LaLanne, or any other food gadget genius with an infomercial. My dad let me use his credit card, and I had no way of reimbursing him.

In early December, Whiskers called and told me to report to Contadino's Pizza after school for my first day of work. I shadowed the main busboy, Gus. I pretty much got the hang of it: clear tables, refill water, and generally help out wherever possible. I was cocksure heading into my first non-shadow day, a busy Friday. I fell behind on the table setting, and Gus had to bail me out. Then I spilled RC on a lady's lap. For my encore, I knocked a basket of bread all over the floor. Mr. Contadino yanked me into the kitchen.

"Let's try back of house for you," he simmered.

He placed me at the dishwashing station and ran through a quick demonstration.

"Think we can handle this?" Mr. Contadino asked.

My first real day at Contadino's, and I was hanging on by a thread. If not for my grandfather's accrued goodwill at the restaurant, Mr. Contadino surely would have given me the boot. I concentrated on doing the dishes to the best of my ability. An hour or so into my dishwashing, Mr. Contadino came in and gave my clean dishes a close examination. He held a plate up to his face, set it down, said nothing, and left the kitchen again.

"Is that good or bad?" I muttered to myself.

"Don't mind Sal," a soft female voice said. "Gruff exterior, tender heart."

LaTonya Davis, the head chef, introduced herself and shook my hand. LaTonya had to be the most elegant pizza chef in Chicago.

"I've been cooking for the Contadinos for two decades, since I was about your age," LaTonya said. "I remember my first week, a total disaster. Felt so overwhelmed. Same goes for Gus. Look at him now. It's part of the industry learning curve."

"Nice to meet you, LaTonya. I'm Crust."

In my head, my voice squeaked like Screech, but LaTonya complimented my manly tone.

"Quite the pipes on you, like James Earl Jones," she said.

LaTonya's golden amber eyes fell on my dish rack.

"You're doing fine, hon," she said. "Hotter water will make it easier to remove the gunk."

LaTonya adjusted the faucet temperature and tested it on her wrist.

"There you go, doll," she smiled. Then she disappeared around the oven wall.

I survived the rest of my shift without further incident. Mrs. Contadino scheduled me for less demanding Monday through Thursday shifts. I hopped a CTA bus straight from school everyday and developed into an efficient dishwasher. I earned my way back into the Contadinos' good graces through effort and reliability. They let me fill in for Gus as head busboy on Christmas Eve, even though it was a busy Saturday. I hardly screwed up at all, save for a dropped fork. After closing, Mr. Contadino poured me a limoncello for the staff Christmas toast. I was officially part of the crew. LaTonya giggled at the way I recoiled after ingesting the potent liqueur.

During my breaks, LaTonya allowed me to hang out on her side of the kitchen. It was a big deal, as she typically shooed staff members away so she could concentrate on her craft. Gus wasn't even allowed back there.

Mr. Contadino prepared the dough fresh daily. LaTonya did the rest. She dusted her work surface with cornmeal and stretched out the dough. The primary purpose of the cornmeal was to prevent the dough from sticking to the peel as the pizza was transferred to the oven. The added texture and flavor were delightful byproducts of the cornmeal. The result was the best pizza crust on the entire North Side.

When she was in her zone, LaTonya was the Picasso of pizza. LaTonya remained poised even when orders piled up or unexpected circumstances disrupted her flow. Her work was fast-paced, but she never seemed hurried.

"Hand me the olives, hon," LaTonya requested.

I did as she asked. LaTonya spread the olive slices evenly across the pie. Even her sprinkling motion was confident and graceful. In the hot, sweaty kitchen, LaTonya's pretty face glistened, framed by a hairnet.

"Onions," she called out.

I leapt from my stool and brought her the bin of chopped onions. LaTonya instructed me to scatter onions across the dough. I hesitated.

Add ingredients? Mr. Contadino warned me to stay away from the food.

"This is my call, my domain," LaTonya insisted. "Do as I say, or get out of my kitchen."

I grabbed a fat handful of onions and shook them onto the dough canvas. The onions clumped here and there, but LaTonya helped me spread them around.

"There you go," LaTonya said. "Not so difficult."

I smiled at her. It must've been a real goofy grin, because she shook her head and laughed. She told me to go sit back on my stool.

"Your shift ended half an hour ago, Crust," LaTonya noted, as she continued her routine. "Why are you still hanging around?"

"Waiting on my ride," I answered. "My dad is taking me to see *Apollo 13*."

"I caught the matinee yesterday. Bill Paxton is divine," LaTonya said.

My dad popped his head into the kitchen.

"Hi Dennis," LaTonya greeted him.

"LaTonya," my dad nodded.

"How do you guys know each other?" I inquired.

"I used to come here with your grandpa," my dad said.

"Years ago," LaTonya smiled.

My dad and LaTonya stared at each other in a way that made me think there was more to the story.

"C'mon Carroll," my dad finally said. "We don't want to miss the previews."

"Enjoy the movie," LaTonya waved.

I interrogated my dad on the ride.

"We used to frequent Contadinos when I was young. I became friends with LaTonya."

"Friends?"

"She's a wonderful gal. Isn't she?"

My dad was starry-eyed. I'd never seen him react to a woman in such a way. I was jealous of his deep connection with LaTonya until I had some time to think about it during the long movie.

What if my dad married LaTonya? She could teach me so much about the art of pizza.

After the movie, I encouraged the scenario.

"You should ask LaTonya out," I told my dad. "She's single."

"It's a thought, son," he grinned. "I don't know, though."

My dad was withholding information. The next day, I asked LaTonya to elaborate on their history.

"Oh, your father, Dennis..." LaTonya drifted into her memory bank. "Mmm-hmm-hmm."

She reached for her apron and stopped answering.

"C'mon," I pleaded. "What's the story?"

"The story is that we kissed one time. But it was only that one time, right here in this kitchen."

"Why only once?"

"Ever read *The Bridges of Madison County*, Crust?"

LaTonya summarized the plot. It was about a farmer's wife who had a brief, passionate affair with a photographer. It didn't sound like my type of book. "I forgot you're not a big reader," LaTonya said. "I'm not saying we had an epic love story, but your dad flirted with me every time he came in to eat with your grandfather. This went on for years. I had a boyfriend, but something about your dad made me happy. One night, there was a terrible collision on the elevated train tracks in the Loop. Your grandpa got called in to provide emergency support. The Contadinos were off attending their niece's wedding in Cincinnati. Dennis was the last patron in the restaurant. It was a bitterly cold evening, and I was stuck closing alone. Dennis offered to help me clean up. I gave him a tour of the kitchen, our eyes met..."

"And you kissed?"

"I shouldn't be telling you all these details," LaTonya said. "Funny how I remember it all so clearly. But, as I said, I had a boyfriend, and I'm not the type to run around. I recall thinking it was the most passionate kiss of my life, yet I ran away as soon as it ended. I avoided Dennis after that, the temptation being too great. Not long after, your dad met your mom. Your mom got pregnant. That was that. I married a different man, not the same boyfriend. The marriage didn't last."

I sensed finality in LaTonya's words. For the rest of my shift, I let her be.

A heat wave baked Chicago the next week, and Contadino's air conditioning went on the fritz. The restaurant closed for two weeks. I used my extra free time to dig into Gloam-pa's recipe book. I turned to one of the last pages. Out dropped the picture I drew of us with our preferred beverages. I felt a happy lump in my throat.

Gloam-pa and his ginger ale.

The flurry of emotion, the heat, and the boredom of two weeks with no job inspired my creative side. I aimed to make my own soft drink from scratch, a hyper-charged ginger ale. I really had no idea what I was doing, so I went to the Chicago Public Library and found a book about the process. I utilized the zest of several fruits, simple syrup, ginger, high-fructose corn syrup, and food coloring.

I had no access to carbonation technology, so I decided my pop would have to go without fizz. I created a pale gold sugar drink I named "Gloam Pop." I adored the flat, syrupy concoction in the way only a mother could love. I believed my dad when he called it "refreshing," even as he washed it down with a glass of vodka. I carried liters of Gloam Pop around in my backpack, in the unrealistic hope that I might run into a Canfield's soda executive on the bus. I believed I had created a masterpiece, and my foolhardy arrogance would soon cost me my job at Contadino's Pizza.

Contadino's reopened in August, salvaging my boring summer. I was thrilled to get back to work, especially since I'd recently earned a promotion. I was Contadino's go-to BOH (back of house) guy, in charge of assembling orders and refilling drinks.

Mr. and Mrs. Contadino took a vacation leading into Labor Day. Gus had been promoted to assistant manager and was left in charge. It was a slow week, so the pressure was minimal. Wednesday after lunch, the soda fountain malfunctioned. I figured it was my opportunity to save the day. I poured pitchers of my homemade concoction and served Gloam Pop to customers. When Gus caught wind of the situation, he was steamed.

"You understand we serve a certain brand of pop here at Contadino's? Not some high schooler's science experiment! What if someone got sick?" Gus yelled.

Gus informed the Contadinos upon their return from Green Lake. Mr. Contadino called me into his office. He was examining a confiscated pitcher of Gloam Pop.

"Crust, I don't know what you are thinking sometimes. This pop you made, it has no bubbles. Pop needs bubbles."

"I'm sorry, Mr. Contadino," I begged forgiveness. "I was trying to help. It won't happen again."

"Our supply guy is not too happy with us," Mr. Contadino said. "And I'm on thin ice with the city about building codes. Can't have the health department in my business too. Sorry, Crust. I have to let you go."

I couldn't speak. I nodded and shook Mr. Contadino's hand. On my way out of the office, LaTonya gave me a warm hug, but I couldn't lift my arms to hug her back. She walked me outside and whispered positive thoughts. I stayed robotic until I got to the car and looked at my dumb face in the rearview mirror. I screamed at myself for being stupid.

I was devastated. Contadino's was my life. Senior year of high school was off to a bummer of a start. I didn't know what to do with myself after school. I'd grown out of baseball cards, and cooking at home no longer provided the same thrill. Great Aunt Mildred urged me to get back on the soft drink horse, but the wounds were still too fresh. I put my soda pop dream on the back burner.

I started hanging out with a girl from school named Alice. She liked the Cubs, which was our initial icebreaker. Alice took me to the Cubs Convention in January. She broke up with me while we waited in line to get an autograph from idiosyncratic Cubs' right-hander Turk Wendell. The line was two hours long, and Alice dumped me halfway through. I had to decide whether to stand alongside Alice in awkward silence for the subsequent hour and get the autograph or leave the line and waste the hour I'd already invested. I stuck it out. The tension between Alice and me must've been apparent, because the superstitious pitcher sensed something was amiss and signed my convention program:

`Hang in there, champ! Turk Wendell`

I was more bored than heartbroken with Alice out of the picture. I moped around the house. It was my last year before I went off to...*college maybe?* I figured I'd spend some quality time with the old man, for his sake. Problem was, my dad's schedule was suddenly unpredictable. He didn't always come home for dinner. He even did stuff without me on the weekends. It was bizarre.

One Saturday, I slept over at Dale Gorman's. Dale's mom woke him up super early for Sunday church, and I walked home while the early birds were still chirping. My house smelled like pancakes. I found my dad at the griddle.

"This is a surprise!" I applauded. "Dad making breakfast! Never thought I'd see the day."

I sat down at the table in front of a place setting. I heard the toilet flush and the bathroom sink turn on.

"I didn't expect you home so early, Carroll," my dad said, as he struggled to flip a pancake.

LaTonya strolled into the kitchen wearing a robe, which she cinched up when she caught sight of me.

"Morning, Crust," she patted my head.

"I invited LaTonya over for a breakfast date," my dad explained.

LaTonya hugged my dad from behind and rested her head on his shoulder while he mishandled another pancake.

"Where do you keep the syrup, Crust?" LaTonya asked.

"Middle shelf, to the right of the sink," I answered.

Once the shock wore off, I had a nice breakfast with my dad and LaTonya. She brought a feminine energy that the house had been sorely lacking. Conversation at the breakfast table seemed more complete and well-rounded than it ever had.

LaTonya's presence at the house became a regular thing. I liked having her around, and she made my dad very happy. LaTonya spent time with me in the kitchen, working on different recipes. We didn't have an oven capable of cooking a proper pizza, but I picked LaTonya's brain for expertise.

One afternoon, I came home from my new part-time job at Play It Again Sports to a mailbox full of responses from colleges. I asked LaTonya if we could open them together. We discarded the rejection letters and weighed the pros and cons of my remaining options. After a thoughtful discussion, LaTonya became convinced that University of Iowa was the school for me.

"Are you pushing for Iowa because *The Bridges of Madison County* is based there?" I asked.

"Crust! I take it you read the book?"

"Picked it up at the library. Not bad."

LaTonya smiled.

"I want to go to Iowa," I said. "Unfortunately, my dad thinks I should stay local and go to culinary school in the city."

"Let me talk to him," LaTonya said.

The next morning, I made eggs. My dad took a big sip of coffee and put his hand on my shoulder.

"Son, I think you should seriously consider the University of Iowa. They've got a great business school. Could prepare you to open your own restaurant down the line."

I glanced at LaTonya, who hid a bursting smile with both hands.

That was how I ended up in Iowa City.

2

Iowa City Pizza Lovers

August 28, 1996. One Hundred Sixty-Five Days Until National Pizza Day

The University of Iowa paired me with a dorm roommate from Naperville, an affluent suburb of Chicago. He had such a fancy name, Evan Fromager III, that I doubted we'd get along. On the other hand, Gloam-pa—who was known to buy wax-lined paper cups of frosty Old Style for strangers from all walks of life at Wrigley Field—once told me a silver spoon doesn't guarantee a stuffed shirt any more than humble beginnings forecast a heart of gold. Nevertheless, I kept a guarded mind on move-in day.

Evan was all settled in by the time my old man and I arrived at Burge Residence Hall to unload my stuff from our Oldsmobile Cutlass. He hopped to his feet to greet us. Evan was a few inches taller than me, about six foot one. He was big enough to make me wonder if he played high school sports. Conversely, Evan's scruffy haircut suggested he might've been the founding member of a garage band.

"Carroll!" Evan welcomed me. "Great to finally meet you, man. How cool is our room?"

"Call me Crust. This is my dad."

"Mr. Crzytok! A pleasure."

Evan pulled on a pair of brand new Air Jordans and followed us down to bring up a load of my junk. I wondered if Evan's good-natured demeanor was a front.

This could just be his act in front of parents.

My dad hugged me goodbye, and I felt a surge of freedom. Evan kicked off his gym shoes.

"Should we order a pizza?" he asked.

"Sure. Know any good places?"

Evan pulled out a Trapper Keeper. Inside, he'd filed menus from every pizzeria in Iowa City.

"Don't laugh," he said. "I did my research."

"This is super well-organized," I remarked. "Monica Geller quality."

I instantly regretted letting the *Friends* sitcom reference slip out. I'd promised myself I would drop that routine, as my obscure TV and movie references often hindered conversations with peers. Luckily, Evan was a fan of the show and even connected with a specific character.

"My motivation comes from more of a Joey Tribbiani place," Evan laughed. "Any organizational skills are simply the byproduct of an intense, never-ending hunger."

Evan and I studied the menus and debated for an hour before finally landing on a place. We pledged to eventually try every pizza in the book. Evan wiped his class schedule off the dry erase board calendar above his bed so we could write out a pizza itinerary. Our first night as roommates was spent eating and planning future food orders.

The next morning, I arose to find Evan hunched over his desk, writing in a blue notebook.

"I made coffee, Crust," he pointed to the pot atop his mini fridge. "Help yourself."

This was no facade of friendliness. Evan was a good guy.

"Not a coffee drinker myself," I said. "Homework already? Classes don't start until Monday."

"Nah, this is my geeky thing," he said. "It's my review of last night's pizza order. Take a look."

Evan's "THREE-O SCALE" was intricate. Every main aspect of the pizza was assigned a numerical grade. The previous night's order earned 42 for crust; 54 for cheese; 66 for toppings coverage; 17 for sauce; and 49 for presentation. Subcategories explained how the overall score was tabulated. For example, the crust's overall score was 42 when factoring in 59 for freshness ; 71 for crispiness; 60 for chewiness; 54 for doneness; 22 for flavor; 29 for bottom crust; 33 for durability; and a wow factor of 11. At the bottom of the scorecard there was space for additional notes. Evan wrote:

```
Drenched with oil, this pie couldn't support a
green onion much less a thick chunk of sausage.
Zilch on pizzazz, this pizza left me wondering why
the cook even bothered rolling out the dough. I'd
label the sauce "forgettable," but unfortunately
its metallic aftertaste will haunt my tongue for
days.
```

One glance at the empty box on our dorm room floor caused my belly to ache. It was a misfire from Cheese & Cheese Pizza Factory, located one town over in Coralville. I patted Evan on the back.

"You're like an official scorekeeper. A pizza statistician."

"To jog my memory," Evan said. "Otherwise, I forget the specifics."

I understood. Chicago Cubs legend Andre Dawson kept a journal of his at-bats with details about each pitcher he faced and every pitch thrown. Evan took a similarly comprehensive approach so he'd never swing and miss on a key order. I wondered how long he'd been tracking his pizzas.

Iowa City's pizza scene proved stellar. Evan's THREE-O scores trended higher and higher as we gathered intel on the best local places. I let him do the math, but Evan sought my input. Within the first month, we zeroed in on our top five pizzerias. The Airliner was the parlor most recommended by students, and the cheesy slices never disappointed. Wig & Pen's phenomenal stuffed crust required a knife and fork. Falbo Bros. was a welcome addition to Iowa City courtesy of Madison, Wisconsin. Sam's Pizza served up thin crust on par with the best in any area code. A&A Pagliai's fed generations of hungry Hawkeyes. It was an Iowa institution for good reason.

Although Evan rated the five pizza joints about equally on the THREE-O SCALE, his infatuation with Pagliai's was undeniable. After all, Pagliai's is where Evan fell in love—not with a pizza, but with a girl.

***

October 3, 1996. One Hundred Twenty-Nine Days Until National Pizza Day

In between our Thursday afternoon classes, Evan and I stopped at Pagliai's for lunch. Weak with hunger as I awaited our Palace Special (sausage, beef, pepperoni, mushroom, and onion), I lost a grip on my large pop. It spilled everywhere. A fellow diner handed me a wad of napkins. She was our age, cute, and affable.

"Holy buckets of Mountain Dew!" she laughed. "Hope they give you a refill."

Evan thanked her on my behalf as I sopped up puddles of Dew with the napkins.

"You betcha," she smiled. "Heaven knows I've tipped over a pop or two in my day."

The folksy lady made a funny face then returned to her seat. Evan tapped my leg under the table.

"Should I ask her to eat with us, Crust?" he whispered.

He took a big sip of ice water for courage. I lifted my legs apologetically so the Pagliai's guy could mop under my feet.

"Are you hungry?" Evan asked the girl.

"Weird if I wasn't. Sitting at a restaurant, reading the menu, and all," she reasoned.

"Yeah, I guess," Evan laughed. "We've got an extra-large on the way if you want to share. I mean, if you want to join us."

Before Evan could finish inviting her, the outgoing blonde was scooching him over in our booth to make room.

"I'm Anna."

I'd seen immediate love in movies before but never in real life. Evan and Anna were certified soulmates. They transformed from strangers to sweethearts over the course of one meal, all because I spilled my pop.

I recognized Anna Sauser as Minnesota nice—a brand of homespun, genuine kindness common among residents of the North Star State. Minnesotans not only offered the sweaters off their backs but also the long johns from under their snow pants.

Anna was a peach. She added instant mirth to our conversation, as she was super funny and self-deprecating. Her Midwest colloquialisms and comically dramatic pauses cracked me up. She proved great company.

Sitting in the booth during that first encounter with Anna, the three of us had no idea we were under surveillance. We failed to notice the loud man with giant feet and his goofy, gangly cohort in the booth behind us, observing our every move; the worker with the mop, lingering; or the busboy who seemed overly invested in refilling our ice water. Evan and Anna were too busy falling in love, and I was naturally oblivious,

3

PIZZA PORTAL

T hroughout history, countless individuals have been blessed with super-talents. Florence Price composed symphonies as a youth. Robin Williams cheered up struggling classmates with impersonations of quirky teachers. Raghib Ismail earned the nickname "Rocket" during eighth grade track practice.

Evan Fromager III dreamed about pizza, which wasn't the most obvious supertalent. Evan didn't hit the ground running like Price, Williams, or Ismail. He was in high school before he even realized his dreams were different.

Evan's power wasn't inherited. He came from a normal, everyday family. Junior Fromager, Evan's dad, was raised in Waterloo, Iowa. Junior attended Iowa State University in Ames, where he met his future wife, Sally Grenville of Council Bluffs, at a Truth and Janey rock concert. Junior and Sally eventually settled in Naperville, Illinois and opened Fromager Records on Loomis Street. The store established a reliable customer base. As music technology evolved, Fromager Records transitioned seamlessly from vinyl records to cassette tapes to compact discs. Sally Fromager made sure the lines moved quickly on Tuesdays when anticipated albums hit store shelves. Legend has it she worked the cash register without a break for five straight hours when *In Through the Out Door* brought Led Zeppelin listeners in through the front door. Sally spent seven uninterrupted hours ringing up Prince fans who poured into the store when *Purple Rain* dropped. She topped that record with nine hours straight appeasing shoppers who feared they'd never land a copy of Michael Jackson's *Bad*.

Junior and Sally's children, Jennifer and Evan, considered the store a second home. The kids reported to Fromager Records after school. Evan became an appreciator of all genres, which enhanced his ability to converse knowledgeably with any fanatic who shopped at Fromager Records. He did his musical homework. Evan listened on his Walkman while traipsing around town. He listened at night right up until bedtime and in the morning as he got ready for school. As Sally and Junior grew more confused with newer forms of music, they could refer younger customers to their son.

"Kris Kross? My son might be able to help you."

"'Achy Breaky Heart'? My son will know who sings it."

"Did you say 'In Utero'? Evan, a customer has a question!"

When Evan's older sister matriculated at University of Illinois in downstate Champaign-Urbana, the Fromagers hired the son of a family friend to help out at the store. Theo was Evan's age and had recently moved to Naperville from Indianapolis. During Theo's first shift, Evan asked if he liked grunge music.

"*Dirt* was the best album of 1992," Theo responded. "That is, if you consider Alice in Chains grunge."

"Good question: Metal or grunge?" Evan pondered.

"Either way, Alice in Chains rocks," Theo said.

Evan made the rock and roll hand signal and sang the refrain from "Rooster" off the *Dirt* album. Theo headbanged. A friendship was born.

The teen duo basically ran the store. Theo was a genius at categorizing CDs. He could name the record company, executive producer, and track listings for every CD he stocked. Evan picked up random CDs and quizzed Theo as they worked side by side.

"OK, Theo. Track four on *Bigger, Better, Faster, More!* by 4 Non Blondes?"

"'Pleasantly Blue,' written by Linda Perry. Two minutes, twenty-eight seconds."

"Dude, you're amazing! How about track six from Da Brat's *Funkdafied*?"

"'Ain't No Thang' featuring Y-Tee. Three minutes, fifty-four seconds."

"Unreal, Theo! Here's a tough one: Which album includes the songs 'Bob,' 'Nature Boy,' and 'Mr. Krinkle'?"

"*Pork Soda* by Primus, self-produced, Interscope and Prawn Song Records. Tracks four, seven, and eleven."

"You should be an MTV VJ, Theo."

Theo never tired of the questions as long as Evan was asking. If a customer overheard the game and chimed in, Evan instinctively diverted the customer's attention. Evan felt compelled to play rodeo clown because of a private conversation he'd had with Theo's mom, who was caring but overprotective. She expressed deep concern about her son's timid nature. She worried about Theo's ability to handle everyday interactions, especially with strangers. Evan promised to head off any potentially awkward conversations.

Theo's house featured a finished basement complete with a Pop-A-Shot machine and a refrigerator full of Gatorades. It was easy to lose track of time in Theo's basement. Theo and Evan stayed glued to the couch, playing Nintendo. Nothing made Evan laugh harder than Theo's tendency to create nonsensical lyrics to go along with games' computerized theme music. Theo sang goofy words that had nothing to do with the game action. Theo's greatest hit, in Evan's opinion, went along with the repetitive *RBI Baseball* melody:

> "*Bob Fomp-te-lon-ski*
> *Oh Bob Fomp-te-lon-ski*
> *Oh Bob Fomp-te-lon-ski*
> *Right now...*"

Bob Fomptelonski was not a baseball player featured in the Nintendo game. Neither was Bob Fomptelonski a person who existed anywhere in the world as far as they knew. Theo created the name out of thin air, and, in the ears of the two friends, the name perfectly matched the rhythm of the *RBI Baseball* theme. Only Theo and Evan found the song even remotely funny, as it was—if they were honest with themselves—quite ridiculous. They played *RBI Baseball* for hours on end and laughed themselves silly.

Friday nights, Evan and Theo counted inventory until long after the store closed. Sally Fromager authorized petty cash so the boys could order pizza.

Naperville, with a population of 100,000, boasted a thriving restaurant scene and plenty of pizzerias. Evan and Theo made it their mission to order and rate every local pizza. They instituted a strict grading system called the "THREE-O SCALE." The lowest rating registered on the THREE-O SCALE was 27, earned by a sausage and green pepper disaster from Dippy's in nearby Plainfield. The highest ever awarded was 88, to a pepperoni pizza they carried out from Al's in neighboring Warrenville. The THREE-O SCALE included variables and conversion charts for deep dish, stuffed pizza, and jumbo slices. Logs of their findings, recorded in simple school notebooks, were filed away in Evan's cubby at the store.

As they plated squares of a well-done mushroom thin crust from Uncle Pete's one Friday night, Evan asked Theo if he ever experienced lucid dreams.

"Can't say I have," Theo responded. "What's it like?"

"Like I'm floating through real environments—but in places I've never been with people I've never met," Evan explained. "The weirdest thing is that it only happens on Pizza Fridays."

"Curious," Theo considered. "Most dreams involve people and places the dreamer knows. Is there an emotion attached? Are you scared? Happy?"

"I feel...a responsibility. And an opportunity to do something good."

"Don't ignore that impulse," Theo said. "Whatever is occurring on Pizza Fridays sounds like more than a throwaway dream."

The next day Evan told Theo every aspect of the previous night's lucid dream in which Evan sat in a kitchen, unnoticed, as a man named Rudy Malnati welcomed diners to Pizzeria Uno, the original home of Chicago deep dish pizza.

"I swear I saw a Navy pilot who looked like a young President Bush," Evan recalled.

"George Herbert Walker Bush completed his World War II training at Chicago's Navy Pier in 1943, the same year Uno's opened. You're somehow time-traveling, Evan."

The concept of time-traveling in his sleep freaked Evan out, but Theo advised him not to overthink it.

"Don't try and figure everything out all at once, Evan. Just experience it. Pay attention to details. Perhaps the purpose will become clear someday."

"It is kinda fun," Evan admitted. "I can't wait to get to sleep on Fridays."

"Do we know for certain it only happens on Fridays?" Theo asked. "Let's eat pizza again tonight."

They made a Saturday night of it at Papa Passero's in Westmont, playing video games and wolfing down pizza. Sure enough, Evan had a lucid dream. He stood by as Gus Guerra served up Detroit-style pizza at Buddy's on the corner of Conant and Six Mile. Customers wore fedoras and fancy dresses. It reminded Evan of a black-and-white photograph of his grandparents. Theo persuaded Evan to keep a dream journal in addition to his THREE-O scorebook.

That Sunday, Theo had a family obligation. Evan ordered a pizza on his own and prepared to drift off into dreamland.

Which pizza mecca will I visit tonight? Philly? New Jersey? New Haven?

Evan woke up disappointed on Monday morning after a dreamless night. He reported the lack of lucidity to Theo after school as they restocked Queensryche albums.

"The pizza was solid," Evan said. "Seventy-nine on the THREE-O. I don't get it."

"You ate alone," Theo said. "Pizza is meant to be shared. Think about your dreams. The purveyors are always serving pizza to others or dining with a group. Eating alone is fine, but it's not the full experience. Sharing good pizza is your ticket to lucid dreams."

The winter of 1995 brought great joy for Evan, as Michael Jordan returned to professional basketball. A meaty portion of Evan's heart belonged to the Chicago Bulls. Evan earnestly supported Jordan's baseball career change because he understood how meaningful the undertaking was to his idol. By February 1995, with no end in sight to the baseball labor strike, rejoining the NBA was the logical move for MJ.

The summer of 1995 brought great gloom for Evan, as Theo's family moved to Lake Geneva, Wisconsin. Fortunately, the drive was less than two hours from Naperville, so Evan could visit at least one weekend a month. Theo missed

working at the record store. Evan pledged to help Theo find equally rewarding employment in the Badger State, something befitting Theo's considerable
talents.

One Saturday, between interviews at un-Theo-worthy Lake Geneva record
stores, Evan and Theo discovered a restaurant called Wily Gene's Pizza Canteen.
"Goofy name," Evan said. "Let's give it a shot, Theo."

The establishment was empty, despite the fact it was noon on a busy summer
lake-town weekend. Evan and Theo tried to decipher the menu, which featured
unorthodox choices:

```
WILY GENE'S SPECIALTY PIZZAS
Orange You Glad I Said Banana Pizza: Orange
chicken, banana peppers
Chili Dog Bath Pizza: Hot dogs, cup of chili
for dunking
I Can't Be Chive It's Not Butter Pizza:
Cantaloupe, Chives, Butter
Wicked Plumber Pizza: Apricots, Spinach -
guaranteed to motivate your digestive system!
Lime Di-Cheese: Lime wedges, cheese from Tick
County cows
Tortoise and Hare: Turtle chocolates, rabbit
meat
```

Theo and Evan looked up from their menus, perplexed by the bizarre choices.
A tired young man in faded blue jeans and a denim jacket appeared at the table.
Everything about the man's physical presence was humdrum. His looks weren't
off-putting or repugnant, but rather simply unremarkable. He had the type of
face that was difficult to capture in one's memory. He spoke without projecting.
Words fell out of his mouth.

"May I take your order?" he yawned.

"Hi, there," Evan greeted him. "Could we get a plain cheese pizza?"

"No special orders," the man said. "The Lime Di-Cheese has cheese on it."

"OK," Evan replied. "Can we get a Lime Di-Cheese with no limes?"

Irritated, the man pointed out a sign on the wall:

Menu Items Only!

"Wily Gene runs a tight ship," Evan quipped. "He's a real stickler, eh?"

"I'm Wily Gene," the man said. "This is my restaurant."

"Oh," Evan was surprised. "I'm Evan. This is my friend Theo."

Wily Gene shifted his weight from one leg to the other with nervous energy.

"There's no way you can make us a plain cheese pizza? It's your place, after all. We're the only patrons. We won't tell," Evan winked.

"I am not above the rules of the business," Wily Gene said. "I'll give you a few more minutes."

Wily Gene made himself scarce until Evan and Theo took the hint and left his restaurant without eating.

That night at Theo's new house, they listened to the latest Bone Thugs-N-Harmony album and reflected on the strange eatery experience.

"What was the menu item after the butter pizza?" Evan asked.

"'Wicked Plumber Pizza,'" Theo answered. "'Apricots, Spinach—guaranteed to motivate your digestive system!'"

They doubled over, laughing until it hurt.

"Gross taste combination," Evan gagged. "How is that description appetizing? Who wants to think about that while they eat?"

"Orange you glad I said banana?" Theo remarked, setting off another round of raucous laughter.

"If you were forced to order one, what would you get?" Evan asked.

"Chili Dog Bath," Theo chose. "Might be decent."

Despite the mockery, Evan and Theo felt sympathy for the clueless restaurateur.

"I should help Wily Gene," Theo half-joked. "Remake his menu."

Evan loved the idea. The troubled pizzeria had the potential to suit Theo's passions and abilities.

The following day, Evan and Theo returned to Wily Gene's Pizza Canteen. The blinds were closed, and a cardboard sign was haphazardly taped to the front door:

OUT OF BUSINESS

Theo shrugged and walked back to the car, but Evan's curiosity about Wily Gene led him around to the back of the restaurant. He peered through a screen door and saw Wily Gene sitting alone, staring blankly at a wall. Evan watched him sit motionless for a solid minute before he knocked on the screen.

"We're closed," Wily Gene said.

"Wily Gene," Evan said. "It's me, Evan. I was here yesterday."

"No refunds," Wily Gene snapped, still not looking at the door.

"Refund? We didn't even eat anything."

Wily Gene stood up and kicked open the screen door. He stared at Evan.

"What do you want?"

"I think I can help you."

"Do you have a time machine?" Wily Gene asked.

Evan gave the ridiculous question careful consideration.

"Beat it," Wily Gene said. "My lease expires in thirty-two days. After this ship sinks, I think I'll try opening a coffeehouse. Seems to be the cash cow nowadays."

Wily Gene yanked the door closed. Evan was undeterred. He pressed his face against the screen.

"Thirty-two days is plenty of time to turn the tide," Evan said.

"Listen, Evan. I sell, on average, about three pizzas per day. I'll need to sell ten times that just to break even next month."

"You're in luck," Evan smiled. "I happen to know a visionary who's in need of a job. He's sitting in my car out front."

"I'm not hiring. Did you not hear me? I'm going belly up."

"What do you have to lose?"

The confidence in Evan's voice gave Wily Gene a shot of adrenaline.

Theo started his new career at Wily Gene's Pizza Canteen a day later. On his very first day, Theo was able to convince Wily Gene to abandon his zany ingredient combinations and get back to basics. Theo called Evan at Fromager Records to share the details.

"Day one, and you're already moving mountains," Evan applauded. "Proud of you, man."

Evan hung up the phone and hit play on the countertop CD player. He bobbed his head to Collective Soul's latest album, but construction sounds forced him to turn up the volume on his boombox. He glared out front window at the site of the future Phantom Wonderstore, a flashy retail outlet that threatened to doom Fromager Records. The five-story Wonderstore boasted endless shelf space for CDs, LaserDiscs, and video games.

Mariah Carey, Jenny McCarthy, and David Schwimmer signed posters at Phantom Wonderstore's September grand opening. On that day, loyal customers made a point of shopping at Fromager Records. Sally and Junior thanked the patrons with free brownies, cookies, and lemonade. The Wonderstore countered with an advertisement in the *Naperville Sun* promoting in-store appearances by Green Day, Gary Sinise, and *Beverly Hills, 90210* heartthrob Jason Priestley. Fromager Records was overmatched.

October delivered Evan an unexpected gift when the Bulls acquired Dennis "The Worm" Rodman from the San Antonio Spurs. The oddball power forward added to the anticipation of Michael Jordan's first full season back with the team. Evan called Theo to talk basketball, but Theo had a surprise for Evan. His new boss had given him a pair of tickets to the Bulls home opener.

On November third, Theo met Evan for pregame pizza at Exchequer on Wabash Avenue in the Chicago Loop. An animated Theo gave Evan a rundown of all the innovations he'd instituted at Wily Gene's Pizza Canteen. Theo researched reliable suppliers across the Midwest that could guarantee consistent quality, from meats to cheeses to vegetables. Wily Gene ponied up the cash for top ingredients and trusted Theo's instincts. The tiny parlor was thriving, even as the busy season wound down, and the sometimes dreaded but economically necessary "Illinois People" ditched the cozy Wisconsin town for the winter. Hearing about Theo's career thrill ride gave Evan's brain a much needed break from the stress caused by the Phantom Wonderstore's shadow. Rodman's Bulls debut was a smashing success, as The Worm pulled down eleven rebounds. Michael Jordan chipped in forty-two points, for his part. The roar inside "The House That Jordan Built" was louder than a space shuttle launch. Theo and Evan screamed and cheered alongside 20,000 fellow fanatics.

Christmas receipts at Fromager Records provided enough of a yuletide boost to give the family breathing room. Evan received a Christmas present in the mail. Theo sent him a bright red Bulls Starter jacket. The note said:

```
To My Best Friend Evan: You're the Jordan to my
Rodman…or vice versa. Stay warm, Theo
```

A docile Midwest wrapped itself in a snow blanket and settled in for post-holidays hibernation. Evan went to school, worked, and watched the Bulls go undefeated throughout January.

On Groundhog Day, Evan ordered a pizza to the store and jammed out to the new album from Stabbing Westward, a local band Theo introduced him to once upon a time. He picked up the phone but got Theo's answering machine.

"Theo, it's Evan. Spinning *Wither Blister Burn & Peel*, and it rocks, dude. I remember you played me Stabbing Westward's song on the *Clerks* soundtrack, back in the day. Anyways…talk soon, bud. Oh, I'm also currently going to town on Giordano's stuffed spinach pizza. Haven't tabulated the THREE-O score yet, but it's hitting the spot."

Evan's February turned dramatic when he attempted to end the relationship with his high school girlfriend, Henrietta, one week before Valentine's Day.

"I don't think we have anything in common anymore," was the line Evan used.

The phrase left too much wiggle room. Henrietta interpreted it as less of a breakup and more of a challenge to start liking everything Evan liked. He appreciated Henrietta's spirited attempts to delve deep into music, the Bulls, and pizza, but her soul wasn't in it. Evan no longer had romantic desires for Henrietta, but he still cared for her as a person. He agreed to continue the relationship until the end of senior year. Henrietta broke it off for good when she learned Evan's availability for prom was contingent on the Bulls' playoff schedule. Henrietta attended the dance with another boy. Evan watched Game 2 of the Bulls and Sonics at Fromager Records.

Evan and Theo lost touch for much of the spring, but Evan knew another Lake Geneva summer was approaching, meaning hang time would be plentiful. He was surprised Theo didn't want to take the train down for the Bulls' Championship celebration at Grant Park. Theo bailed on a planned road trip to Detroit to catch Alice in Chains in concert. Evan tried pleading with him.

"If not for me, Theo, do it for Alice in Chains!"

Theo would not budge. Evan handed off the concert tickets to his sister and her boyfriend.

To keep his mind off the frayed friendship, Evan focused on getting ready for college.

Junior and Sally Fromager gave their blessing when Evan opted to enroll at their alma mater's in-state rival, the University of Iowa. Naperville was close enough that Evan could make a day trip for summer orientation. He borrowed his sister's old Camry and hopped on I-88 West. As he neared Rochelle, he flipped through a CD booklet and selected *American Recordings* by Johnny Cash. He knew the album was produced by Rick Rubin; Theo drilled that fact into Evan's head. He remembered the day Theo noted that "A Boy Named Sue" was written by poet Shel Silverstein. Evan subsequently dropped the tidbit on country music fans galore at Fromager Records.

Evan detoured towards Wisconsin. An hour and fifteen minutes later, Evan pulled up at Theo's house. Theo's mom welcomed Evan and offered him a Capri-Sun. She directed him down to the basement, where Theo was playing Nintendo.

"Game of *RBI Baseball*? For old times' sake?" Evan suggested.

Theo agreed and blew the dust from the cartridge. Theo dominated the game from the start, stealing second and third base with the Cardinals' Vince Coleman.

"Geez. Give me a chance to get warmed up, Theo," Evan joked.

Theo hid a smile. Evan sensed his old pal was warming up to the unannounced visitor.

"You excel at video games; you're a music encyclopedia," Evan extolled. "And now, of course, you're the Master P of the pizza industry. I drove past Wily Gene's Pizza Canteen on the way here."

"I'm no longer affiliated with Wily Gene's Pizza Canteen. I quit. Time to move on and try something else," Theo said.

Evan understood that geniuses like Theo constantly required new challenges.

"That's cool," Evan nodded. "Happy to help you find your next thing."

Theo paused the game.

"I don't need you to babysit me anymore. I can speak for myself. I can find a job by myself," Theo said.

"We're friends, Theo. Friends offer to help."

The game resumed in uncomfortable silence, aside from the familiar *RBI Baseball* theme music. To break the tension, Evan started singing Theo's "Bob Fomptelonski" lyrics.

"I think I outgrew that song," Theo discouraged. "It stopped being funny a long time ago."

Evan and Theo finished the game without another word.

"Welp," Evan said. "I oughta hit the road."

"Good luck at Iowa," Theo managed, before resetting for a one-player game.

Dazed and dejected, Evan slunk away.

A month of self-examination followed.

Am I guilty of steamrolling Theo?

Alanis Morissette dominated the radio airwaves with "You Learn," and the pensive yet sanguine tune convinced Evan to take a lesson from his deteriorated friendship with Theo and move forward. He found solace in preparing for one of life's biggest changes: college. The day he received his dorm roommate assignment in the mail, Evan made a vow.

I'll be a good friend to you, Carroll Crzytok, first and foremost.

4

STUDYING FOR MIDTERMS

February 6, 1997. Three Days Until National Pizza Day

Weekends started Thursday on Big Ten college campuses, unless your Economics professor scheduled a midterm examination on a Friday, as mine did. On the bright side, I had a study buddy because Evan had an Environmental History midterm. We bundled up for the walk across campus to the Main Library.

"Someday my beard will protect my face from winter weather," I said, measuring my facial growth in the mirror. "Two weeks since my last shave, and still pretty sparse coverage."

"Keep your chin up," Evan said. "It'll grow in."

"Is your coat insulated?" I asked.

Evan's most treasured possession was his pullover Bulls Starter jacket.

"Winter-tested," Evan nodded. "Besides, it's snowing. It's not as cold when it's actively snowing."

Evan stated the temperature factoid with the conviction of WGN weatherman Tom Skilling. We put on our backpacks and hit the hallway. The 4400 floor of Burge buzzed with energy. Dorm room doors were propped open to encourage visitors. Dudes coordinated plans for a night out on the famous Iowa City Pedestrian Mall.

"Bulls lost their sixth game last night, Evan," Prankster Hank shouted. "Looking less and less likely they match last year's seventy-two wins."

"Rodman returns from his suspension soon," Evan reminded him. "That'll help right the ship."

"Yeah, he shouldn't have kicked that cameraman," Prankster Hank nodded. "Why did he do that?"

"That's Rodman for ya," Evan shrugged. "Take the good with the bad."

Prankster Hank was our dorm's resident maestro of merriment. As his name suggested, Prankster Hank lived for practical jokes. His sense of humor was puckish, and his gags were harmless hijinks.

Prankster Hank beckoned us to his doorway. He grabbed the telephone from his room and stretched the wire out into the hallway, where he put his ear up against the closed door of his next-door neighbor, Jerry. Prankster Hank smiled and dialed. We heard the loud dorm phone ring inside the door.

BRRRRRRRRRRRIIIIINNNGGGGG!!

Jerry answered.

"Hello, Jerry, it's Hank. Listen, I'm making a fluffernutter sandwich, and I'm short on marshmallow fluff. You wouldn't happen to have any, would you? Hey, I'm actually at your door now..."

As Jerry opened the door to greet Prankster Hank, he dropped the phone away from his face, revealing a mess of marshmallow fluff all over his ear. Jerry realized he'd been pranked and applauded the quality gag.

"Marshmallow fluff on my phone!" Jerry laughed. "Well done, Prankster Hank. You got me!"

"You're a good sport, Jerry," Prankster Hank said, handing him a gift certificate for a free burrito from Pancheros. That was a Prankster Hank signature—if he got you good, he gave you an immediate gift as a reward for being cool.

"Panchies!" Jerry exclaimed. "My favorite. Thanks, Prankster Hank!"

Jerry wiped his ear with a towel and held his parting gift in triumph. Prankster Hank set down the phone and accompanied us down the hallway.

"Hitting up The Airliner for a slice. My treat, if you guys are hungry," Prankster Hank offered.

"Can't join you, Prankster Hank. Studying for midterms," Evan said.

"Midterms stink," Prankster Hank pronounced. "Second semester is flying by. See you dudes later."

The Main Library's primary study floor was the place to get homework done, with its hundreds of tables and the hush of silent concentration common in libraries full of college students cramming for tests. Evan spotted my favorite part-time library page, Trivia Trixie, restacking shelves atop a ladder. She was wearing ripped jeans and her gray Bayside Tigers T-shirt.

"Ready to throw down, Crust?" Evan smiled.

I steadied my heartbeat and approached the base of the ladder on wheels. Without looking down, Trivia Trixie knew I was there.

"Hey, Crust. Did you know Tony from *Dazed in Confused* is the same kid who played Daryl in *Adventures in Babysitting*?"

I was dazzled by the depth of her pop culture knowledge.

"I was not aware of that," I said.

Trivia Trixie glanced down, and I caught sight of her hazel eyes. She stood five foot five and frequently volunteered to restock the top shelves because she appreciated the rare glimpse of people from above.

"Did you watch *Seinfeld* tonight, Crust?" she asked.

"Yes! The Martin Van Buren thing was hilarious. Eighth President."

We both held up eight fingers simultaneously.

"Jinx," she called.

"You can't jinx a hand signal," I argued.

"I beg to differ," Evan strode up beside me. "The bylaws of jinx don't exclude sign language."

Trivia Trixie gestured at Evan in agreement.

"Fine," I sighed. "I owe Trixie a pop."

"I don't drink pop," Trivia Trixie said. "And you're supposed to stay silent until someone says your name."

I nudged Evan, hoping he'd bust me out of jinx prison.

"Sorry, can't help you," he laughed. "Should I say his name, Trix?"

"I'll let him off the hook," Trixie smiled. "After all, he's a man of few words."

She teased me with the beginning of my name until finally releasing me from the spell.

"Crrrrrrrrr....ust."

I was glad to speak again because I had a follow-up question.

"How come you don't drink pop? Super strict parents or something?"

"No, there were always soft drinks in the fridge. Didn't appeal to me."

"What did you drink?"

"Water, I guess," Trivia Trixie thought about it. "Or milk."

I liked learning more about Trixie, who rarely talked about herself.

"I owe you a water," I said. "Or a milk."

"Make it a Pie Milkshake from Hamburg Inn."

"Deal."

Evan, my main wingman, knew I harbored a crush on Trivia Trixie. He constantly attempted to facilitate hangout opportunities outside the library.

"Anna is doing research at the observatory tonight," Evan mentioned. "I'm surprising her with a pizza from Pagliai's. You're welcome to join us, Trix. You too, Crust."

Trixie didn't bite.

"Eh, thanks for the invite. Wig & Pen is my preferred pizza. Besides, I'm catching a midnight movie later with my Scenic Art classmates. The original *Star Wars* is back in theaters."

I remembered a trivia question I'd researched to try and stump Trixie.

"Hey, got one for you Trixie: Can you name the pizza place from *Home Alone*?"

"Too easy, Crust," she answered. "Little Nero's."

Trivia Trixie noticed the book in Evan's hand, *Last Chance to See*, by Douglas Adams and Mark Carwardine. She recommended he check out the audio version. Evan left his coat and book bag with me at a table and wandered down the hall to the Media Room, which offered audio cubicles with attached headphones. He reemerged thirty minutes later with sleep indents on his face.

"How was the book on tape?" I asked.

"Interesting stuff," he said, before admitting he dozed off after fifteen minutes.

Evan glanced down at his jacket and peeled a Post-it note from the back. He held up the yellow sticky note, which had a pepperoni pizza drawn in blue pen.

"Nice doodle, Crust," he said.

"That's not one of mine. I only draw sausage pizza," I said.

"Not a Crust original? Who left it on my coat?"

I glanced around the study room and rubbed my stubbly chin. I didn't spot any likely suspects. Evan assumed Prankster Hank was somehow involved. He wadded up the Post-it and threw it in the trash.

5

— • —

ASTRONOMER ANNA

Sunday brunches were a tradition for the Sauser family of Eden Prairie, Minnesota. Ten times per year, the meal was served in LOT #3 outside the Hubert H. Humphrey Metrodome. The Sausers never missed a Vikings home game: two preseason, eight regular season, plus the occasional playoff home game. Uncle Dolph drove the RV, Uncle Holger iced the beverage coolers, and Brandt Sauser, Anna's dad, was the grillmaster.

Brandt charred bratwurst and hot dogs to perfection. If his wife, Debbie, requested her burger a little pink, Brandt served it up a little pink. For a medium-rare porterhouse, Brandt's internal timer told him the precise moment to tong the steak onto the plate and let it rest. Brandt's allegiance was to charcoal. He arranged the coals to provide both direct and indirect heat. The indirect heat was for chicken thighs, ribs, and Brandt's signature grilled onions. Brandt hailed the onion for its versatility. Lesser tailgaters neglected Mother Nature's flavor bulb, but Brandt refused to take it for granted. No other plant demanded tears in exchange for its essence. Brandt considered the sting of onion eyes the price of admission. He halved his onions, added his homemade marinade, and swaddled the halves in aluminum foil. After an hour of indirect heat, Brandt chopped and presented his onions. Young Anna loaded her hot dogs with the tasty topping. She watched in disbelief as her cousins bypassed the caramelized garnish while simultaneously appreciating the fact that there would be leftovers. She knew the leftover onions would be used on Brandt's famous grilled pizza on Monday. Anna was a good eater who never turned down pizza, no matter the combination of toppings. Her personal favorite, however, was pizza with onions only. To Anna, there was something unique about the simplicity of onion pizza. It became her thing.

Anna's mom, Debbie, was a woman of considerable knowledge. On family camping adventures, Anna tried to find constellations that Debbie couldn't name off the top of her head.

"How about over there, Mom?"

Debbie would set her Milwaukee's Best in the cupholder of the folding chair and look to the sky where her daughter was pointing.

"Puppis," Debbie identified. "Which is Latin for 'poop deck.'"

"You're making that up. Seriously? Poop deck?" Brandt laughed.

"Seriously," Debbie giggled. "Don't look at me. I didn't name it."

"The poop deck constellation," Brandt chortled.

Debbie's expertise was hard-earned. She graduated with Distinction from the United States Naval Academy and served as a U.S. Navy quartermaster for nearly a decade before accepting a job with the Department of Natural Resources back home in the Land of 10,000 Lakes.

Anna wanted to be like her mom. She read books, initially of the science fiction classification. Anna soon realized she preferred facts over fantasy and gravitated to the non-fiction section of her school library. Her favorite book was *Ice Chunks and Dust: How Saturn's Rings Formed,* by Professor Homer Carson. Professor Carson made complex topics understandable without dumbing down the material. Anna also noticed a subtle, wry, and self-deprecating sense of humor that Carson slipped into his work. She admired his writing. The biography page noted that Homer Carson was a professor at the University of Iowa Department of Physics and Astronomy. Anna set her sights on becoming a Hawkeye so she could study under Professor Carson.

Anna had five older brothers: Alan, Carl, Jim, Gary, and Doug. The boys were named after the "Purple People Eaters," the fearsome Vikings defensive line of the late 1960s and early 1970s. Anna looked up to her brothers and they, in turn, adored and protected her. They let Anna tag along as they chased frogs, ding-dong-ditched neighbors, or flooded the backyard in the winter to make an oblong hockey rink.

Debbie Sauser did her best to ensure Anna got special attention as the youngest child and the only girl. They decorated Anna's room together, complete with a half-dozen posters of Anna's crush, tennis star Andre Agassi. One Saturday a month, Debbie and Anna went to Minneapolis for a Jucy Lucy lunch, followed by a stop at a museum or a stroll through a summer street festival.

Anna worked as a babysitter, and any money she didn't save was spent at Little Books on the Prairie—the cutest bookstore in Eden Prairie. A kind, elderly couple owned the shop and stocked the non-fiction section for their favorite young customer. Anna spent hours browsing titles or reading her purchases at the tiny round tables near the back exit.

Debbie's sister, Peggy, moved to the Twin Cities as Anna was entering high school. Peggy attended beauty school and worked the front desk at Fabulous Dan's in St. Paul. Her goal was to open her own beauty salon. As Aunt Peggy practiced styling Anna's yellow hair, Anna picked up on the fact that her aunt was awaiting a financial settlement owed to her by her former employer. Anna wasn't privy to the details of the case, but it was apparent Aunt Peggy had been ripped off in some way, shape, or form. Even though Peggy was only getting a fraction of what she was owed, it was a decent enough chunk of startup capital to finance her dream salon.

Debbie and Peggy toured retail locations for lease in The Cities. Debbie liked a spot near the Guthrie Theater, but Peggy leaned toward a storefront facing Como Park. They debated the options as they stopped at Peggy's apartment. Peggy's roommate had signed for an important piece of mail, a certified letter.

"The check finally arrived," Peggy celebrated.

"Open it up!" Debbie said. "What are you waiting for?"

Peggy carefully unsealed the envelope but found no check. The correspondence informed her of a legal roadblock. No payment was forthcoming. Debbie held her sister as she cried tears of frustration but not tears of ultimate defeat. No sooner had Peggy's cheeks dried than the sisters swiveled to a new business plan. Debbie and Brandt's front room would become Peggy's studio. Brandt supported the idea and even suggested a clever name for his sister-in-law's business: Moonlight Glam—based on fictional Minnesota doctor/baseball player Archie "Moonlight" Graham from *Field of Dreams*.

Anna was overjoyed to have her aunt working out of the Sauser home. She never once heard Aunt Peggy moan about being shortchanged by the law. Anna's curiosity boiled over during a family game of Boggle. She wanted to know what transpired with Peggy's former employer.

"What's done is done," Aunt Peggy dodged the topic.

Anna wasn't satisfied with the non-answer and pushed for more information. Peggy held up the board game's plastic hourglass timer.

"Once all the sand goes through, it's game over. Until somebody shakes the dice and starts a new game."

"What happens when other people don't play by the rules?" Anna asked. "If someone smashes the hourglass to pieces?"

Peggy thought about it for one second.

"I'd buy a stopwatch," Peggy answered.

Brandt, Debbie, and Anna's brothers laughed at Peggy's one-liner. Anna grimaced.

"Buck up, Anna," Peggy said. "Your favorite candy bar is a Milky Way, right?"

Anna nodded. Peggy offered food for thought.

"The inventor of the Milky Way suffered from polio, a debilitating disease, when he was a boy. He had to sit inside while his brothers worked the family farm. And I'm sure he was down in the dumps about it. But while he stayed indoors, he watched his mom dip chocolates and learned how to do it. Then he grew up and invented the Milky Way. Every unfair circumstance has a hidden opportunity, if you're able to keep your wits."

Peggy figured the key to expanding her customer base was to tap into the male population. Men, Minnesota men in particular, tended toward old-fashioned barber shops. Peggy sought to redefine men's style. Fortunately, she had five handsome nephews with thick heads of brown hair to act as her guinea pigs. One summer Sunday, with all the brothers home from their respective colleges and jobs, Peggy requested her nephews' assistance. Alan, Carl, Jim, Gary, and Doug reported to Aunt Peggy's studio after dinner. Ninety minutes later, Anna heard a commotion. She rushed down to Peggy's studio, following the sound of her aunt's jubilance. There sat Alan, Carl, Jim, Gary, and Doug. The outermost inch of the brothers' dark hair was bleached, as if they'd each been coronated with crowns of blonde.

"I call this style 'frosted tips,'" Peggy declared.

"I absolutely love it!" Anna smiled. "You all look so cute!"

Alan, Carl, Jim, Gary, and Doug glared at their little sister.

"I know you boys don't aim to be trendsetters," Peggy said. "But this is a cutting-edge look. I really think this could be the new thing."

Five sturdy Minnesota chaps with frosted tips helped Anna move into Currier Residence Hall in Iowa City in August of 1996. Debbie took a Polaroid of the six siblings, which Anna immediately pinned to her bulletin board.

6

— · —

ANNA'S BIG DISCOVERY

February 6, 1997, Ten O'Clock At Night. Still Three Days Until National Pizza Day

After prepping for his midterm at the library, Evan picked up a pizza from Pagliai's and brought it to Van Allen Observatory. Evan emerged from the elevator on the seventh floor. Anna waved him over to her workstation.

"My boyfriend brought me a pizza! You're so thoughtful, babe."

She kissed Evan on the cheek.

"Your face is ice cold, Evan," Anna remarked. "Below zero out there, eh?"

"Your kiss warmed me up," Evan smiled.

"That's why they call me 'Hot Lips,'" Anna joked.

"You're kidding, but I might start referring to you as 'Hot Lips,'" Evan chuckled.

"Fine with me, Frosty Cheeks," Anna winked.

Anna cleared space on the desk for the pizza. Evan noticed a large group of astronomy club members huddled around the telescope.

"Is there a meteor shower or something? Did someone spot a UFO?" Evan wondered.

"Funny you ask," Anna said. "There's an anomaly in the western sky, hovering over Iowa, not far away. We're racing to identify and classify the thing. Hence all the hullabaloo. Uff-da!"

A passing astronomy student offered Anna congratulations.

"You made the discovery, Hot Lips? That's a big deal!" Evan celebrated.

He hugged Anna with such enthusiasm that he nearly lifted her off the ground.

"Thanks, Ev, but it was a team effort. I happened to be on watch at the right moment."

"You're too modest, Anna," Evan said, before realizing he might be in the way on a busy night. "You need me to clear outta here, babe? Let you do your work?"

Anna appreciated Evan's self-awareness. She kissed him again.

"Take some pizza to go," she said. "There are paper plates in the kitchen."

Evan grabbed napkins from the seventh floor kitchen, but he couldn't find the paper plates. He searched the cabinets above the sink. Professor Homer Carson entered, carrying a serving tray of carne asada and rice.

"Professor Carson," Evan greeted him. "I'm Evan, Anna Sauser's boyfriend. We've met once or twice."

"Evan, of course! My wife made plenty of carne asada. I hope you're hungry."

"No, thanks. I'm here to surprise Anna with a pizza."

Professor Carson glanced around the kitchen before he whispered, "I hate to point this out, Evan. But I fear you may have forgotten said pizza."

Evan smiled and told the professor the pizza had already been delivered to Anna's desk.

"I see," Professor Carson adjusted his mustard sport coat. "Quite an accomplishment for that young lady, the discovery she made tonight. You should be proud of her, Evan."

"I am. She's exceptional. I'm a lucky guy."

"It'll be an all-nighter for the Astronomy Club," Professor Carson said. "Better cancel my morning tee time at Finkbine."

"You play golf in the snow?"

"I was being facetious, Evan."

Professor Carson swung an imaginary golf club.

"Hey, any idea where you keep the paper plates, Professor?"

"Good question, Evan. I can locate galaxies twelve billion light years away, but I can't find a darn thing in this kitchen."

7

Gloam Pop Revival

J.R. Grappler, my lab partner in Food Science class, was a brilliant chemistry enthusiast. I told him about my abandoned aspiration to create a soft drink, and J.R. couldn't resist taking up the challenge. We reserved lab time to work on a new formula for Gloam Pop. I leaned on his knowledge for the science stuff. My role was lab assistant. I also designed a flashy black and gold label. J.R. zeroed in on the desired taste but still wanted to perfect the coloring.

"Not quite gold," J.R. assessed. "Too pale. Carbonation seems on point, though. Does it feel like the right amount of bubbles, Crust?"

I drank from a test tube to sample the product.

"Effervescent," I nodded.

"Remember when Urkel ingested a potion and turned into a smooth-talking ladies man?" J.R. laughed.

Like me, J.R. was a fan of *Family Matters*.

J.R. requested the beta-carotene. As I fetched it, I bragged about growing up in proximity to the *Family Matters'* house.

"It's across from Wrightwood Park. You gotta come visit this summer, J.R. I'll show you."

"You act like it's a cross-country visit. Northwest Indiana is basically the South Side of Chicago," J.R. said. "Drive down to Hammond, and I'll take you to State Line Pizza. Best Italian sausage in the tri-state area."

"Strong words," I cautioned.

"I stand by the claim. Come get a sausage pizza this summer and see for yourself," J.R. said.

J.R. added beta-carotene to the mix until our beverage was the correct shade of gold. I taste-tested the product one last time and gave it my seal of approval. The formula for Gloam Pop was complete.

We canned several six-packs, then called it a night. I kept J.R. company while he waited for his Red Route bus back to Slater Hall. I thanked him for making Gloam Pop a reality.

"Anything for my lab partner," J.R. nodded. "Are you coming to the dual meet tomorrow, Crust?"

"Absolutely! Golden Gophers versus the Hawkeyes. I'll be cheering you on, J.R.!"

J.R. Grappler was not only a scientific prodigy, he was also a four-time Indiana state champion wrestler. His fraternal twin brother, Mike, was an accomplished wrestler as well, earning two state titles. Scholarship offers rolled in from schools across the Midwest. J.R. chose Iowa because of its wrestling prowess and chemical engineering department. Mike accepted a full ride to University of Minnesota, where he jumped up a wrestling weight class to heavyweight, the same as his brother. J.R. was preparing to wrestle Mike in a real match for the first time.

"Brother versus brother on the mat. As a wrestling fan, I'm psyched," I said.

That was when J.R. spotted an enormous footprint in the snow.

"Abominable Snowman?" J.R. joked.

We admired the yeti-sized print until his bus arrived

8

CLOWNFOOT AND THE MALAMUTE

I hustled back to Burge to catch Siskel and Ebert on *Late Night with Conan O'Brien*. Midway through Conan's interview with the movie critics, I muted the television to train my ears on a bizarre sound coming from the hallway.

Whoosh.

Whoosh.

Plenty of weird sounds echoed through the hallways of a freshman dorm, but this one stuck out. The pattern was familiar, but I couldn't put my finger on it.

Whoosh.

Whoosh.

I rolled out of my bean bag chair, crawled across the floor, and peeked under the door. I spied a giant pair of Reebok Shaq Attaq Pumps striding past. I rose to my feet and swung open the door. The hallway was empty and eerily quiet.

"Prankster Hank? Is that you?"

Whoosh.

Whoosh.

I followed the whoosh to our floor's trash room and opened the door, where I came face-to-feet with the big Reebok Pumps. They were attached to a stout, red-haired gent laid out on his back. He wore a puffy blue coat, red mittens, and a shark tooth pendant.

"Are you the garbage man?" I asked.

"No, I'm Clownfoot. I ran in here thinking it was the stairway exit."

"What size shoe do you wear, Clownfoot?"

"Twenty-three. Same as Shaquille O'Neal."

"Cool shark tooth. Is it real?"

"Found it on Wailea Beach in my home state of Hawaii."

I helped Clownfoot to his feet, and we walked to my room. Clownfoot removed his mittens and rolled up his coat sleeves. His arms were as hairy and red as his head.

Clownfoot inquired about Gloam-pa's compass, which I wore around my neck as a pendant.

"It belonged to my grandfather," I said. "The same grandfather I named my soft drink after."

I handed Clownfoot a can of Gloam Pop. He opened it and took a sip.

"Not bad!" he said. "But I'm not here to sample soda pop. I tracked you down to make you the offer of a lifetime."

"Are you with Columbia House?" I asked. "Because I already got eight CDs for a penny."

I showed him my copy of *Jock Jams, Volume 2.*

"Listen!" Clownfoot yelled. "This isn't some trivial CD club! It involves an entity far more consequential: pizza."

I gave Clownfoot my undivided attention.

***

Meanwhile, Evan trekked up Jefferson Street, cradling a meal's-worth of pizza between a protective shell of paper plates. He crossed paths with a lanky upperclassman who appeared underdressed in a long sleeve, vest, and 36 Crazyfists ball cap. The guy pointed a gangly arm at Evan's to-go plate.

"What's for dinner?" the stranger wondered.

"Pagliai's," Evan answered.

"Yum, that makes me hungry," the skinny stranger patted his flat belly. "Pizza sounds good."

"Pagliai's is closed for the night, but Falbo's is open 'til three on weeknights. I recommend the supreme. It'll hit the spot," Evan advised.

"You sure know your pizza," the stranger said.

Evan inquired about the guy's lack of winter gear, but the stranger downplayed the snowstorm. He said it paled in comparison to the winters he experienced growing up in Anchorage, Alaska, where he traversed the frozen tundra as a delivery boy for Pizza Man. His dispatcher nicknamed him "The Malamute" as a nod to his sled dog mentality.

"Pizza in Alaska," Evan imagined. "Delivery by snowmobile?"

"No, dude," The Malamute laughed. "We have paved roads in Anchorage. I delivered in my dad's Chevy Silverado."

"Never been to Alaska. Obviously."

"Go to Pizza Man if you ever visit. The crust is sweet, with the ideal balance of crunch and chewiness..."

The Malamute's voice trailed off as he reminisced about his hometown pizza. Evan figured the conversation had come to a natural conclusion.

"Welp, have a good one. Go Hawkeyes," Evan said.

"Wait, Evan," The Malamute said. "What did you think of my sketch? I'm no Michelangelo, but I can draw pizza."

"*You* left that on my coat at the library? Why?"

"Well, Evan, you strike me as a pizza savant. I've got eyes and ears in every Iowa City pizza place. My ring of Connoisseurs noticed your ordering habits—noteworthy for a freshman, both in terms of frequency and variety."

A frosty crosswind ripped down Jefferson Street. Evan clamped down on his paper plates to prevent his meal from blowing away while The Malamute remained unbothered by the blustery weather. Evan was flattered to be recognized as a pizza aficionado but understandably reluctant about trusting a goofy stranger who'd been studying his eating habits from afar.

"My roommate is a big part of the equation," Evan said.

The Malamute was way ahead of him.

"Totally. Crust is the Joe Pesci to your Robert De Niro. My associate is meeting with Crust as we speak. And we'd be fools to omit Astronomer Anna, the Nicole Kidman to your Tom Cruise. She's a bonafide pizza authority, and we need her help. The future of pizza as we know it is at stake. If we don't act, the entire town—and soon the entire country—might suffer the same fate as Blandville."

"Blandville sounds, well, bland," Evan said.

"It didn't used to be," The Malamute sighed. "Until it was infiltrated."

The Malamute sensed Evan's hesitation.

"Detroit-style pizza looks pretty good, doesn't it?" The Malamute asked. "I bet you wanted to try a piece."

Evan froze.

Did The Malamute read my dream journal?

"I had the same dream you had, Evan. Back in high school, I brought a pizza home from work to share with my cousins. That night I had the most realistic dream. Thought I was losing my mind. That was before I learned there were others who dreamed the way I did."

"There are others? How many?"

The Malamute handed Evan a business card with his address.

"Swing by our apartment after Anna finishes up at the observatory tonight. All of your questions will be answered. Pizza will be provided. Please take this seriously, Evan. I believe you have what it takes to lead our coalition into the twenty-first century."

With his message delivered, The Malamute mushed away through the snow.

9

— • —

A SAMPLE OF SECRET PIZZA

February 7th, 1997, Two O'Clock In The Morning. Two Days Until National Pizza Day

Evan and I scooped up Anna from Van Allen Hall and hiked over to Johnson Street. The Malamute welcomed us inside the two-bedroom apartment he shared with Clownfoot. The carpet was freshly vacuumed, and the front hallway was lined with photo collages, film memorabilia, and Groundhog Day ornaments. The Malamute led us on a brief tour, during which he apologized when he noticed Clownfoot's foot powder sitting on the bathroom sink. The tour concluded in the TV room, where Clownfoot lounged beneath a framed *Above The Rim* movie poster featuring Tupac Shakur and Marlon Wayans.

"Greatest basketball movie ever made," Clownfoot proclaimed.

Anna squeezed in between Clownfoot and Evan on the couch. I reclined on the La-Z-Boy. The Malamute set an unmarked pizza box on the coffee table. The aroma triggered my appetite. Before he let us dig in, The Malamute held up a VHS tape.

"Have you ever seen *E.T.*?" The Malamute inquired.

"Late to start watching *E.T.*," Evan said. "I've got a midterm tomorrow."

"We're not watching *E.T.*," Clownfoot interjected. "We assumed you've all seen *E.T.* The Malamute was using it as a point of reference."

I enjoyed film analogies, as movie talk reminded me of Trivia Trixie.

"Remember how they hid E.T. to protect him?" The Malamute asked. "In a similar way, we protect pizza."

"Think of me as Elliot, E.T.'s best friend," Clownfoot said.

Clownfoot's statement ignited an argument. After four years of living together, Clownfoot and The Malamute bickered like siblings. The topic of this particular disagreement may have been frivolous, but the longtime roommates debated with the intensity of Lincoln and Douglas.

"First off, Clownfoot is not Elliot. I'm Elliot," The Malamute declared. "Clownfoot is Elliot's older brother, Mike."

"I don't want to be Mike," Clownfoot whined.

"Would you rather be Drew Barrymore?" The Malamute offered.

"Her character name is Gertie," Clownfoot said. "Fine. I'll be Gertie."

Anna got a tremendous kick out of the quarrelsome duo, yet she felt compelled to move the proceedings along.

"Ditch the movie analogy, gentlemen. Kinda getting stuck in the mud," she noted.

"Astronomer Anna is right," The Malamute agreed. "Let's watch the video."

The Malamute popped the tape in the VCR and hit play. A rudimentary logo appeared on screen for *Connoisseurs of the Circle Cuisine*. The homemade movie began with a map of Italy and a voiceover:

Pizza was originally the food of the working class.

"Is that your voice, Malamute?" Anna asked. "Adorable!"

"Yes," The Malamute whispered. "Listen closely."

The first scene featured The Malamute dressed as a chef. Clownfoot played the King of Italy. The Malamute's voiceover described the action on screen.

Pizza as we know it today was perfected in the 1880s by Naples cafe owner Raffaele Esposito. Raffaele used

oil from an olive tree blessed by Pope Pius IV. Raffaele
made sauce from San Marzano tomatoes grown in the
soil bordering Mt. Vesuvius. Italian commoners devoured
Raffaele's pizza after long days toiling in the orchards.
Word of Raffaele's pizza spread across the region.

In 1889, Italy's King Umberto traveled to Naples. Upon
sampling Raffaele's pizza, the king became enamored
with the peasant cuisine. He demanded that Raffaele
become his personal chef, forcing him to abandon his
cafe and serve his pizza only to royalty. For a decade,
he served pizza to the ruling class. However, deep down
Raffaele felt pizza was for everyone. Raffaele began
sneaking away from the castle at night to feed pizza to
commoners. The late night deliveries went on until King
Umberto found out about the secret pizza service and
imprisoned Raffaele.

At that point in the homemade movie, Clownfoot shifted roles to play
Raffaele Esposito's son, Raffi Jr. The Malamute's voiceover explained:

From behind bars, Raffaele Esposito directed his son
Raffi Jr. to deliver the blessed olive tree to his friend
Gennaro Lombardi in America. The king's soldiers kept
a close watch on Raffaele's family, meaning Raffi Jr.'s escape would require a distraction. He waited until the an-
nual flight of the starlings, when thousands of birds filled
the air. As the starlings caused their seasonal ruckus,
Raffi Jr. slipped away and boarded a ship destined for
New York City. Gennaro Lombardi appreciated the olive

tree gift and helped Raffi Jr. find work digging New York City's subway tunnels. Gennaro later opened Lombardi's Pizza and hired Raffi Jr. to work nights alongside Gennaro's son George, a mozzarella cheese aficionado. Raffi Jr. saved up money and decided to travel west. He visited Philadelphia, Cleveland, and Detroit. West of Chicago, he stopped at a water-powered gristmill on Salt Creek. Graue Mill is where Raffi Jr. developed an appreciation for cornmeal. He learned of a farm in Iowa, where an uncanny supply of corn originated...

The VHS tape turned to static, then cut to a recording of an MTV interview with Tupac Shakur.

"Clownfoot! You taped over the ending!" The Malamate growled.

"My bad," Clownfoot admitted. "This is the interview where Tupac talks about his very first job as a cook at Round Table Pizza."

The Malamute's interest was piqued.

"Really? Tupac made pizza?"

"My theory is that's why he faked his own death: to open a pizzeria called Makaveli's somewhere in the Caribbean," Clownfoot posited. "Being a pizza chef was a happy time in Tupac's life. He wanted to recapture that feeling."

"As much as I want to learn more about Makaveli's Pizza, I'm consumed by the fact that our guests won't get to see the rest of my film," The Malamute said.

I reassured The Malamute that we got the gist of the story. Anna complimented his acting.

"Thank you, Anna. I mean, I'm no Tom Hanks, but maybe someday," The Malamute beamed.

"Now can we eat?" I asked. "I'm ravenous."

"What kind of pizza is this?" Evan inquired.

The Malamute leaned in close.

"Secret Pizza," he whispered.

"Secret Pizza?" Evan questioned. "Never heard of it."

"That's because it's a secret," Clownfoot said.

The Malamute revealed that he and Clownfoot were members of a coalition, the Connoisseurs of the Circle Cuisine.

"I'm the Chief Connoisseur," Clownfoot said. "The Malamute, as Secret Pizza Steward, is the leader of our brigade. This honor is bestowed upon only those born with the preternatural ability to open the Secret Pizza portal."

Anna's expression told me she shared my skepticism. Evan, on the other hand, listened with intent.

"Every time I eat pizza, my dreams are so tangible and intense," Evan related. "I thought I was crazy at first..."

That was the moment I started to believe in Secret Pizza. Something in Evan's tone convinced me it was real.

The Malamute explained that, as Seniors, he and Clownfoot needed to find worthy successors. He wanted Evan to become the next Secret Pizza Steward, with Anna as his Chief Connoisseur.

Before he allowed us to partake in Secret Pizza, The Malamute requested a moment alone to meditate. He excused himself and left the room to find his zen. While we waited for The Malamute to return, Clownfoot suggested we try to guess his favorite pizza topping.

"Uh...sausage?" I asked.

"No," Clownfoot said. "Think way more outside the box."

"Pineapple?" Evan guessed.

"You think just because I'm Hawaiian I like pineapple on my pizza?" Clownfoot sneered.

"I'm sorry, Clownfoot," Evan apologized. "I didn't mean to insult you."

The Malamute overheard the dustup and returned to the room to try and calm his roommate. Clownfoot's huff persisted.

"I happen to be allergic to pineapple," Clownfoot scowled. "My throat closes up."

"Which would be a nice break for the rest of us," The Malamute plugged his ears.

"Shut your face, Malamute!" Clownfoot yelled. "It's a serious condition."

"I apologize. Poor attempt at humor. Trying to lighten the mood," The Malamute retreated. "Evan didn't know you're allergic. He didn't mean anything by it."

"I know," Clownfoot relaxed. "It's all good, Evan. I get worked up sometimes."

Clownfoot offered Evan a low-five to bury the hatchet.

"My favorite topping is ham, by the way," Clownfoot added.

"Ham. Great," The Malamute nodded. "Will you be quiet now so I can find my zen?"

Clownfoot zipped his lips. The Malamute closed his eyes to concentrate. Once he located his zen, The Malamute pulled a piece of Secret Pizza from the box and passed it to Evan, who took a bite and passed it to Anna. Anna took a bite and passed it to Clownfoot. Clownfoot took two bites.

"Save some for Crust, Clownfoot," The Malamute scolded.

"There's a rotation," Clownfoot argued. "Bite, bite, pass."

The Malamute rolled his eyes as Clownfoot finally passed me the big slice. I took a bite, and my tongue started tingling. Intense pizza flavor washed over my tastebuds. Entranced, I passed the slice to The Malamute, who glanced around the table before he took a bite.

The instant The Malamute bit into the Secret Pizza, I was transported. Suddenly, I was eleven years old again, sitting with Gloam-pa and my dad at our neighborhood pizza place. Gloam-pa asked for a sip of my RC. It was more distinct, genuine, and natural than any dream. It felt as if I was experiencing it in real time all over again.

***

I awoke in our dorm room eight hours later. Anna was sitting on the edge of Evan's bed, recounting her vivid dream.

"Felt like I was living in a fuzzy, warm memory. I flashed back to the year of the big Halloween blizzard. My dad made pizza. My brothers and I shoveled the walk so the neighbor kids could trick-or-treat. I felt wonderful and happy."

"Same type of thing for me," I said. "Surrounded by family and at peace."

"How about our fancy new Steward?" Anna asked. "Didja have sweet dreams, honey?"

Anna tickled Evan. Evan giggled and wiggled away.

"Stop," he squealed. "Different for me. I traveled back through history."

"Was it cool like *Bill & Ted's Excellent Adventure?*" I inquired. "Or dark and ominous like *Bill & Ted's Bogus Journey?*"

"I visited Raffaele Esposito's kitchen in 1880s Italy," Evan said.

"Wowzers. I thought we were gonna wait and travel abroad together junior year," Anna deadpanned.

"Seriously," Evan laughed. "It was like I was there. I feel like it's the same type of dream I've always had after consuming pizza, only much clearer."

Evan, Anna, and I had taken the first step towards becoming official Connoisseurs of the Circle Cuisine.

"Secret Pizza was super trippy and all," Anna said. "But raise your hand if you still don't know exactly what we're protecting or how we're supposed to protect it."

All three of us threw our hands in the air.

"First, we need to recruit additional Connoisseurs," Evan said. "Once we do that, The Malamute will give us a complete rundown of our responsibilities."

"Trivia Trixie would get a kick out of the whole secret society whatchamacallit," Anna suggested.

"Totally! Trix would be a fantastic addition," I seconded. "Prankster Hank and J.R. Grappler both love pizza too."

"Three good prospective Connoisseurs right off the bat," Evan said. "We'll run it by them after the wrestling meet. You got the tickets, Crust?"

I pointed to the wrestling tickets pinned to Evan's poster board.

"Cool," he said. "See you at the arena after my midterm. You're coming to the meet, right Anna Bear?"

"You betcha! I'll be decked out in black and gold!"

10

—— ◆ ——

Connoisseurs: The New Class

February 7th, 1997, Three O'Clock In The
Afternoon. Thirty-Three Hours Until National
Pizza Day

Iowa diehards packed Carver-Hawkeye Arena for the dual meet. We crammed into the student section and screamed our lungs out in support of our wrestlers. Prankster Hank waved a sign depicting a Hawkeye with a helpless Gopher in its beak. Anna and Trixie pumped foam fingers in rhythm with the fight song.

The highlight of the afternoon was undefeated freshman sensation J.R. Grappler's match against his twin brother, Mike. Mike Grappler wanted to show the world he was on the same level as his more decorated brother. Mike converted an early takedown off a leg attack to grab an early lead. Mike's momentum ended abruptly when J.R. skipped out of a subsequent attack and swung his legs around his brother's body like a gymnast gliding over a pommel horse. J.R. pinned Mike to earn the victory and clinch the dual meet for the Hawkeyes. Emotion overcame both brothers as they embraced on the mat.

Ron and Shirley Grappler, in town to watch their sons wrestle, invited all of J.R.'s friends to Sam's Pizza for a post-meet meal. Mike Grappler received special permission from Minnesota's coach to spend the weekend in Iowa City with his brother.

"Thank you all for coming out to support the team," J.R. said. "I wanted to also take a moment to congratulate Anna on her discovery last night! Evan said it might put her in the running for the Gordon Meyers Amateur Achievement Award."

"Ope!" Anna blushed. "Somebody's been bragging about his astronomy geek girlfriend."

Evan kissed her on the cheek.

"I can't help it, babe. You're so cool."

Mike Grappler studied the menu and proposed that we order Sam's Special (sausage, pepperoni, mushroom, onion, and green pepper).

"Can't go wrong with Sam's Special," Evan concurred. "Scores in the high eighties on the THREE-O SCALE."

Mr. and Mrs. Grappler awaited an explanation. Anna finally spoke up.

"Evan rates every pizza he eats based on a complex number scale."

"J.R. and I used star ratings when we were kids," Mike Grappler recalled. "Pretended we were food critics."

"Dad burned a frozen pizza, and we gave him zero stars," J.R. laughed.

"He was so mad!" Shirley Grappler giggled.

"I still blame the faulty instructions on the box," Ron Grappler smiled. "Twenty-five minutes at 450 degrees was too much heat!"

After we polished off three Sam's Specials, Shirley and Ron ordered a round of calzones for the hungry group of college students, then paid the bill and hugged the twins goodbye. Mr. and Mrs. Grappler had a long drive back to Indiana. The rest of us stayed at Sam's to await the impending calzones.

With the finest freshmen pizza minds in Iowa City at one table, Evan seized the moment and pitched the gathered pizza buffs on becoming Connoisseurs of the Circle Cuisine. He described the mysterious alliance tasked with protecting an otherworldly realm of pizza.

"It's called 'Secret Pizza,'" Evan said. "I'll warn you it's more than simply a scrumptious meal. It's an out-of-body experience; it's a psychedelic phenomenon; it's a supernatural portal that unlocks your happiest pizza memories."

"Cool, I'm in," Prankster Hank said as he munched on a breadstick.

"That easy? No follow-up questions at all, Hank?" Evan asked.

"Does it cost money to join?" Prankster Hank inquired.

Evan shook his head.

"Then I'm in," Prankster Hank said. "Free pizza club."

"Free pizza club?" J.R. considered. "When you put it that way, I'm in too."

"Super!" Anna said. "Trixie?"

"You had me at 'scrumptious,'" Trixie smiled.

Mike Grappler wanted to participate as well, but we weren't sure if Golden Gophers were eligible. Evan dispatched me to the payphone in the back room of the restaurant. I didn't have any change, so I called collect.

Rinnnnnnngggg.

Rinnnnnnngggg.

"Hello?" Clownfoot answered.

Automated voice: You have a collect call from:

"Crust."

Automated voice: Will you accept the charges?

"Yes," Clownfoot sighed.

Our call was connected.

"You called collect?"

"1-800-COLLECT," I clarified. "Saved you a buck or two."

"Whatever," Clownfoot huffed. "Did you assemble a squadron?"

I listed the new team members: Prankster Hank, Trivia Trixie, J.R. Grappler, and Mike Grappler.

"The Grappler who wrestles for Minnesota?" Clownfoot paused. "I don't know about a Gopher becoming an Iowa City Connoisseur. Let me confer with The Malamute."

Clownfoot held his hand over the receiver, but I could hear a muffled conversation from my end:

"*Mmmmm bmmmph grmm hmmmph crust hmmmph kmmmdrrrrrr nnnnsota.*"

"*Dmm lbbbbrrrt fnnnd ebbbbbbbelll?*"

"*Dnn el frrrfeee yazzzzzmmmm.*"

"*Guzzz soppa gild.*"

"*Bzzz a hzzz.*"

Clownfoot uncovered the phone to give me the ruling.

"The Golden Gopher may accompany you on the mission, but only in an unofficial capacity. That means you're still short on numbers. Add one more Connoisseur to your squad."

I strained my brain to think of another worthy candidate, when a familiar face emerged from Sam's restroom.

"Hey Chill Gil!" I shouted. "Want to join a group of food fanatics on a mission to protect a century-old pizza recipe?"

"Sure, Crust," Chill Gil responded. "Sign me up."

I returned to my phone conversation with Clownfoot and added Chill Gil to the roster.

"Chill Gil? Never heard of him," Clownfoot said. "He's not on our radar."

"Keeps a low profile, but believe me, he gets it. Gil ends each and every night with a slice or two from Falbo Bros."

"Very well, Crust. If you vouch for him, your word is enough for me," Clownfoot said. "Orientation will commence tonight at Bo-James Bar."

An announcement came over the loudspeaker as Clownfoot hung up on me:

Sam's Pizza asks that our diners give a warm welcome to television's Jaleel White! Thank you Jaleel for choosing Sam's Pizza while you're visiting Iowa City!

I dashed back to the dining room to catch a glimpse of the *Family Matters* star. Unfortunately, all I saw was Prankster Hank doing the Urkel dance around the hostess he'd persuaded to make the false announcement.

"Got me, Prankster Hank," I laughed. "I really thought Urkel stopped in for a calzone."

Prankster Hank handed me a bag emblazoned with the ABC-TV logo. I was elated when I opened it to discover my gift.

"An Urkel koozie! Thank you."

"To keep your Gloam Pop cold," Prankster Hank hugged me. "Congrats on finalizing the formula. You should be proud, Crust."

I pulled a can of Gloam Pop from my coat pocket and slid it into the koozie. "Fits like a glove," I smiled.

***

We had a few hours to kill before Connoisseur orientation, so everyone went their separate ways to recharge. I arranged a game of pool with Chill Gil at Joe's Place to brief him on the whole Secret Pizza saga. He only had one follow up question:

"I can still eat Falbo's whenever I want?"

My double thumbs-up satisfied Chill Gil.

"Combo, corner pocket," he called before he cracked one ball into another to execute a savvy combination shot.

Chill Gil circled the table, turning his Green Bay Packers hat backwards and scrutinizing the stripes and solids through his thick-rimmed glasses. The pool cue skimmed deftly between his knuckles, striking the cue ball with authority and precision. The pool table was his miniature Lambeau Field, and he was Desmond Howard finding the seam.

Chill Gil ran the table until it was time to head over to orientation. The Malamute and Clownfoot beckoned us to a back booth at Bo-James. The Malamute handed each of us a syllabus, along with a manual titled *Connoisseurs' Compendium*—a Secret Pizza handbook Clownfoot typed up for recruits. Because he was only observing, Mike Grappler wasn't issued his own manual but was permitted to glance at his brother's copy. J.R. inquired as to why a pizza club opted to meet at Bo-James, a hangout famous for burger baskets.

"Our freshman year we held meetings at pizza parlors. Inevitably, random pizza halfwits would overhear our discussions and try to sidle up and join the conversation," Clownfoot said.

"They'd overhear *you*, loudmouth," The Malamute clarified.

"I refuse to apologize for speaking with passion," Clownfoot rejected the criticism.

"One guy tried to lecture *us* on ordering pizza well-done," The Malamute recalled.

"Arrogant buffoon!" Clownfoot chortled. "As if we'd never heard of well-done pizza! Only a budlacker would have the gall."

"What's a 'budlacker'?" I asked.

Clownfoot directed me to the glossary of the *Connoisseurs' Compendium*. A budlacker was defined as:

```
a pizza rookie; an individual lacking taste buds
and prone to preferring subpar pizza
```

Clownfoot and The Malamute excused themselves and bellied up to the front bar to enjoy cold beers, leaving us newbies to page through our manuals in the back of the restaurant. Trivia Trixie highlighted the introduction:

```
Pizza can be a connective tissue for families,
friends, and communities. The Circle Cuisine, when
sliced and pulled apart, brings people together.
Connoisseurs honor generational traditions and
patronize neighborhood restaurants. We share food
and make memories.
```

J.R. Grappler found an ominous passage:

```
Beware the onslaught of unworthy foes who seek to
annex Secret Pizza and bastardize it for profit.
```

A Connoisseur who discounts the turpitude of the
green-eyed adversary endangers his or her brethren.

"To quote David Hume: 'The corruption of the best things give rise to the
worst,'" Chill Gil said.

"Is he the guitarist who left Metallica to form Megadeth?" I asked.

"You're thinking of Dave *Mustaine*, Crust," Evan whispered in my ear.
"Chill Gil is quoting a Scottish philosopher from the eighteenth century.
Megadeth rules, though, for the record."

Prankster Hank pointed out the section that differentiated Stewards from
Connoisseurs:

Secret Pizza is meant for the people, served with
dedication and love to neighbors, colleagues, and
kin. Secret Pizza is not an entity or brand unto
itself. On the contrary, its magical properties
can be applied to pizzas from any worthy oven.
Take, for example, the five modern legends of Iowa
City; all are authorized purveyors of Secret Pizza.
Card-carrying Connoisseurs may obtain Secret Pizzas
from any of these neighborhood establishments. The
catch is, Connoisseurs can only experience the
transcendental effects of Secret Pizza as part of
a ritual in the company of a Pizza Steward or Pizza
Steward Emeritus. (A Pizza Steward graduates to
Emeritus status once he finds a worthy successor
and transfers current status to the next Steward.)
There shall be only one active Pizza Steward on
campus at any given time.

Early Century Iowa City Pizza Stewards:
George Gallup 1923-1925

Mildred Augustine 1925-1927
Daniel Friend 1927-1931
Milton Hammersby 1931-1936
Jane Potts 1935-1937
Thomas Williams 1937-1938
Grant Wood 1938-1941
Filippo Greco 1941-1943
Mary O'Connor 1943-1945
Helen Friedman 1945-1948
William Snodgrass 1948-1952
Yu Kwang-chung 1952-1956
Jean Seberg 1956-1957

Before voluntarily leaving office in 1957, Steward
Seberg decreed that the true identity of the Pizza
Steward would henceforth be kept under wraps, for
the good of the cause and the safety of all
involved. Therefore, the list of Pizza Stewards
from 1957 to present are listed by clever monikers:

Simon Sings 1957-1961
Sioux City Steve 1961-1964
Mop Top 1964-1968
Tommy Anchors 1968-1969
Jack Jump 1969-1973
Winner Tut 1973-1976
Bison Tennyson 1976-1980
Hero Zuonie 1980-1984
Cap Ten Luau Banjo 1984-1988
Bunny Rogers 1988-1992
Left Said Fred 1992-1993
The Malamute 1993-Present

Evan Fromager, the Pizza Steward-in-waiting, had no nickname. J.R. Grappler suggested "Evan Fro" as an homage to the Pearl Jam song "Even Flow." Evan's reaction was lukewarm, which Anna found strange because Evan adored rock 'n' roll witticisms. She noticed Evan fidgeting, in the subtle way that only a significant other can recognize. Luckily, Anna was skilled at using her wit to alleviate Evan's stress.

"Can't believe I'm dating the future Steward," Anna riffed. "If only my high school friends could see me now. I feel like pizza royalty. Call me 'Princess Pie.'"

Evan laughed, which briefly eased his anxiety about taking on the role. Despite Anna's efforts, Evan's self-doubt resurfaced a minute later.

"Why me?" he asked. "Why not Crust, Anna, or Hank? Or anyone else? You all know as much about pizza as I do."

"Take it as a compliment, babe," Anna said. "These seniors sense something special in you."

"We've got your back, Evan," J.R. reminded him. "You're not doing this alone."

The Malamute and Clownfoot returned to gather our impressions of the information and ascertain whether our crew would prove a dedicated bunch. Trivia Trixie requested a clarification.

"The syllabus says prospective Connoisseurs must solve puzzles in order to find 'The Source.' What is The Source?"

"The Source is the epicenter of Secret Pizza," Clownfoot replied. "Hallowed ground. Solve riddles and piece together a map. Prove yourselves worthy of protecting Secret Pizza by locating The Source."

The Malamute decreed that J.R. Grappler, Prankster Hank, Chill Gil, and Trivia Trixie would be issued personal challenges within the next twenty-four hours.

"If the four tasks are completed to our satisfaction, clues will be earned. An additional riddle, also containing a clue, will be issued to your designated Chief Connoisseur, Astronomer Anna. Put all five clues together and find The Source, where you will face your ultimate test as a team."

"Do we wait by our phones for these challenges?" Prankster Hank asked.

"Nope," Clownfoot said. "We'll find you."

"Creepy," Trivia Trixie said. "But fun. I'm kind of excited now."

Clownfoot and The Malamute invited us around the corner to The Airliner so everyone could experience Secret Pizza. They even included Mike Grappler, although only as a spectator. Cloris the waitress winked at The Malamute and showed us to a table set for ten. I pulled a can of Gloam Pop from my coat pocket, but Cloris caught me.

"Ope! No outside drinks, hon," Cloris said. "What is that, Natty Ice?"

"Gloam Pop," I said. "We make it ourselves. Want to try one?"

I held up the can for Cloris to inspect.

"I'm good," she refused. "And I'm sorry, but you'll have to pocket your Gloam Pop and order a Coke or something."

I complied and ordered a regular pop. When our pizza arrived, I waited for The Malamute to begin his zen ritual, but he called an audible.

"Let's give Evan the wheel," The Malamute decided. "Ready to take these guys on a ride, young Steward?"

"I don't know how," Evan said.

"Sure you do," The Malamute responded. "You're a natural. We picked you for a reason. A Pizza Steward is simply a conductor. Harness the energy of Secret Pizza and let it combine with the capacity of pizza aptitude amassed around this table. The passion of your Connoisseurs ignites your innate power. Close your eyes and let it happen."

Evan gave it the old college try but quickly opened his eyes in frustration. The Malamute tagged in Clownfoot to inspire the struggling apprentice. Clownfoot steadied Evan's shoulders like he was Hawkeye football coach Hayden Fry delivering a pep talk to a freshman quarterback.

"I want you to imagine Secret Pizza as a bolt of lightning," Clownfoot said. "This table is the DeLorean and you're Doc Brown. All you gotta do is connect the wires and let the electricity flow. You've seen *Back to the Future*, right?"

"Of course," Evan took a deep breath. "I can do this."

Evan tuned out the noise from neighboring tables. He thought about his sixteenth birthday party at Barnaby's in Northbrook. Evan envisioned the thin crust with the edges pinched so it cooked up extra crispy.

"Eighty-seven," Evan mumbled.

"What did he say?" Clownfoot wondered aloud.

"Eighty-seven," I deciphered. "He rates all pizzas numerically."

Evan's eyes opened wide, and he invited us to begin. As the apprentice Steward and the rest of us dug in, I soared off on another expedition through personal history. This time I landed in the kitchen at Contadino's, where I shared an unclaimed takeout pizza with Gus and LaTonya. LaTonya presented me with my own Contadino's apron as an official member of the team.

The rest of the prospective Connoisseurs raved about their first rides. J.R. celebrated with long-lost youth wrestling teammates at State Line Pizza. Trivia Trixie found herself back home in Parma, Ohio at Antonio's Pizza And Spaghetti. Prankster Hank fetched his mom's purse so she could pay the delivery guy from Leonardo's in Cedar Rapids. Chill Gil warmed up at Yountie's in Monroe, Wisconsin.

All of our recruits pledged allegiance to the cause. The team was set.

11

TRIVIA TRIXIE OF OHIO

When Trixie Moses was five years old, a movie crew picked her family's house in Cleveland as the setting for a Christmas film. Paul and Dorothy Moses moved their three young children to Trixie's grandparents home for a week in June while their house was transformed into a holiday wonderland. The film hit theaters that November. Illuminated and decorated, the family home looked glorious onscreen. *The Plain Dealer* wrote an article about the home and quoted Paul Moses. Local TV stations featured the famous house on the evening news. Paul and Dorothy Moses' home was the pride of the neighborhood. Trixie's classmates asked if she knew the characters from the movie.

"It's all make-believe," she explained to fellow kindergartners. "They only used the outside of our house."

Movie money upped the ante for the family's Christmas festivities. Paul and Dorothy hosted a gathering of friends and extended family for dinner at the famous house. Life imitated art, as the film inspired the decor, and Dorothy served thematic dishes. Santa Claus was extremely good to the Moses children.

The film left theaters in mid-January, and the hubbub died down. Paul became a self-proclaimed expert on filming locations, pointing out inconsistencies while the family watched TV.

"*Newhart* isn't filmed in Vermont," Paul reminded the kids on a weekly basis.

The Christmas movie came out on VHS the following autumn. The family house became a destination for far-flung fans of the film. Carloads of travelers stopped at the house to take pictures. Bold visitors walked right up to the door to ask for a tour. Paul started charging five dollars per person. He and Dorothy decided to redecorate the inside to resemble the movie set. They earned over five hundred dollars from walkthroughs. The windfall inspired Paul and Dorothy to turn their home into a full-time tourist attraction. Paul sold T-shirts and hats. It was Christmas all year long at the Moses house, as tourism wasn't limited to December. The city of Cleveland erected a street sign directing visitors toward the famous dwelling. Local accordion legend Frankie Yankovic took the tour and posed for pictures. Business was so good that Paul quit his sales job.

Trixie and her two younger brothers adjusted to growing up in a movie museum. By the time she was ten years old, Trixie was a bonafide tour guide.

Dorothy and Paul doubled down on their investment, purchasing two neighboring homes for an expanded tour space and a spacious gift shop. Construction was completed in September of 1990. That same year, a new Christmas movie was set to debut in theaters. Paul caught a preview of the film and dismissed the premise.

"Parents forget to bring the kid on vacation? Sounds like a dud."

Home Alone turned out to be a Christmas blockbuster and a cultural phenomenon. Yuletide movie tourists spent their traveler's checks in Winnetka, Illinois, instead of at the Moses' compound in Cleveland.

Construction bills came due as customers grew scarce. Financial stress contributed to Paul Moses' near-fatal heart attack in the winter of 1992. The Moses family sold the properties and left the city. They settled into the friendly suburb of Parma. Paul recovered, and the family survived the change in lifestyle. Trixie swore she would never watch another Christmas movie.

Parma's most famous resident was Ettiore Boiardi, better known as Chef Boyardee. A signed photo of Chef Boyardee hung on the wall at Antonio's Pizza And Spaghetti. The autographed picture captured Trixie's attention one evening as the Moses family waited for a table. Curiosity led Trixie to the library to research the man behind the brand name. She found a newspaper article about Ettiore Boiardi. Trixie grew fascinated with Boiardi's journey, from Italy to Cleveland and into the annals of food history. Her deep dive into Boiardi's life inspired a thirst for minutia.

A few weeks after Trixie entered high school, Dorothy took the three Moses children to Burgess Dinner Theater for a stage performance of *Bye Bye Birdie*. Trixie liked the show and loved Burgess' Cleveland-style pizza, with its grooved, doughy crust and provolone cheese.

Trixie chose to spend her birthday at Burgess that December, even though Paul warned her it would feature a Christmas show. Trixie backed off her anti-Christmas stance for a joyous retelling of *It's a Wonderful Life*. The Moses family stood in the lobby post-show, full of pizza and good cheer. The theater manager asked if they enjoyed the show. Trixie raved about the performances but condemned the drab set.

"You reused the set from *Bye Bye Birdie*. We do better work in my freshman stagecraft class."

Dorothy apologized for her daughter's brash critique. The manager blamed a shortage of stage workers and offered Trixie a part-time job. With her mom and dad's approval, Trixie accepted.

The family stopped at Ruby's Video Store on the way home so Trixie could rent the original film version of *It's a Wonderful Life*. She studied the backgrounds and details. The next day Dorothy took Trixie to Michaels to purchase arts and crafts. Trixie showed up for her first day of work with a heavenly set of wings. The actor playing the angel was touched by the gesture.

Trixie excelled at stagecraft. She dabbled in hostessing duties at Burgess as well. Her decisive demeanor and ability to assess customer needs made her an asset in the front of the house. By her sophomore year, Trixie was basically managing the show business side of Burgess.

One day, her manager asked her to deal with a crew member named Martin.

"He's got a hole in his right shoe. If it's a money issue, we'll buy him new shoes," the manager said.

Martin met with Trixie for a private chat.

"You wanted to see me, Trixie?" Martin asked.

Martin was the same age as Trixie but attended a different school. Trixie never noticed the hole in his shoe. She knew he was a reliable worker, however.

"Yes, Martin. It's about your uniform."

Trixie stood up from her chair and kissed Martin on the lips. He kissed her back.

"What size shoe do you wear?" Trixie asked.

"Eleven," Martin answered.

"Everyone is getting new uniform shoes. They'll be in your locker next week," she said.

Trixie stole another kiss from the cute stagehand, then marched over to her manager and told him to supply the entire staff with new shoes. The manager fretted about the cost, but authorized the purchase.

Trixie and Martin maintained a secret romance until the logistics of separate high schools caused them to drift apart. There were no tears when things ended, only a meaningful hug in the same office where they first kissed. Trixie liked Martin very much but realized it was merely puppy love. She appreciated him for being such a sweet first boyfriend.

When Trixie wasn't working or doing homework, movies and TV helped her unwind. Her appetite for films was unparalleled. Trixie regularly rented four or five movies per weekend. If a classmate named a movie, chances were Trixie had seen it and could quote dialogue.

Paul Moses recorded every primetime show so Trixie could watch the programs after work. At breakfast, Paul quizzed his daughter on the specifics of each episode. Even when Trixie was wiped out and wanted only to sleep, she stayed up late watching shows so she didn't fail her dad's morning quiz.

Trixie's senior year of high school began two weeks before Paul's most anticipated new show of the decade: *The Drew Carey Show*. The sitcom was set in Cleveland. Overall, Paul approved of the portrayal of their hometown, even though the show was filmed elsewhere. Trixie decided to make Wednesday her permanent day off so she could watch Drew Carey with her dad.

***

February 8, 1997, Midday. Twelve Hours Until National Pizza Day

I woke up early, shortly before noon, because I signed up for a tour at the UI Museum of Art. I liked to sketch and appreciated art, but it was an enchanting tour guide who drew me to a museum on a Saturday.

"My name is Trixie Moses. Welcome to the Alma Thomas exhibit."

Trivia Trixie shared a quote attributed to the noteworthy American artist. I tried to pay attention but lost my concentration when Trixie flashed a cute smile midway through the delivery of the line. It was something about creative art being timeless. Trixie led a group of tourists around the gallery and spoke eloquently about each painting. She took her job seriously.

Trixie wrapped up the tour, and I lingered to applaud her "helmsmanship." (It was a term I'd recently learned in an elective class about conquistadors.)

"I like that word," she smiled. "Thanks, Crust. Which was your fav—"

Trixie stopped mid-sentence and beelined toward a painting called *Snoopy Sees Earth Wrapped in Sunset*. A yellow Post-it note was stuck to the frame. The note had a sketch of a pizza and the following words:

> MOVIES AND TV
> FOR YOU AREN'T TRICKY
> WIN THE TRIVIA CONTEST
> HELD AT MICKY'S

Trixie disapproved of sticky notes left on invaluable works of art. Nevertheless, she accepted the challenge. I offered to accompany Trixie to Micky's for the trivia contest. She politely declined.

"Feels like a solo mission, Crust. They don't call me 'Trivia Trixie' for nothing."

12

— • —

THE NEXUS

I critiqued my interaction with Trixie as I made my way down Clinton Street.

Next to the bookstore, a banner welcomed guests to a Soda Pop Expo.

How did I not hear about this event? The Daily Iowan never mentioned a Soda Pop Expo arriving in Iowa City.

A mascot in a foam pop bottle outfit waved me inside. He slammed the door shut behind me, leaving me seemingly alone in a spacious conference room.

"Crud," I said.

"Crust?" a voice called out from behind me.

It was J.R. Grappler. I was glad to see him.

"They tricked you too, Crust? I should've known the Soda Pop Expo was a mirage."

An upperclassman in a three-piece suit entered the room pushing a chalkboard on wheels. He picked up a piece of chalk and wrote The Nexus on the board in cursive, although he had to erase the x once and rewrite it to make it more legible. He wiped his hands high in the air, then checked all sides of his body to ensure chalk dust had not sullied his suit. Satisfied, he invited us to take a seat at the table.

"I am Lionel Dwellings of Nexus Trainee Team 3-1-9. Apologies for the misdirection. Our research indicates it can be advantageous to utilize creative recruitment techniques."

"More deceptive than creative," J.R. grumbled. "Save the preamble. Why are we here?"

"Gloam Pop is not for sale," I emphasized.

Lionel Dwellings' haircut wiggled when he chuckled.

"This has nothing to do with your soda brand. Zero interest there," Lionel assured me.

"Oh, good," I said, humbled.

"However, your scientific endeavors, combined with your zest for pizza, made us believe you'd be candidates to join our association."

"I'm already in one pizza coalition. Not sure I want to join another," I said.

"Ah, yes. The Connoisseurs," Lionel nodded. "The Nexus is, let's say, more advanced. Allow me to show you."

Lionel led us through a metal door into an immaculate test kitchen. The oven was state-of-the-art and every surface was stainless steel. It was clean, organized, and as sterile as an operating room.

"Welcome to The Nexus," Lionel said, mimicking the momentous inflection of the old man from *Jurassic Park*. "Should you join our ranks—and rest assured we want both of you, Crust and J.R.—access to the latest in kitchen technology is one of the many perks. You'll hold the title of 'Intrepid.' As an Intrepid, you'll connect with a network of bright young food minds from around the world. You'll be given the freedom to experiment and help us come up with innovative ideas like our stromboli-crust pizza. Plus, a lucrative full-time job offer awaits upon graduation. If that isn't enough, you'll also be given one of these."

Lionel showed us his laminated ID card. It identified him as a "PIP."

"What's a pip?" I asked.

"A backup singer," J.R. quipped. "Or a British kid with great expectations."

"Very clever, J.R.," Lionel attempted to laugh like a regular person. "*P-I-P* stands for 'Pizza Intrepid Passport.' It entitles the holder to unlimited free pizza in over one hundred twenty countries."

"How many countries are there in the world?" I asked.

"One hundred ninety," J.R. estimated.

"Pretty widespread pip saturation," I congratulated Lionel.

Lionel removed his coat and rolled up his shirt sleeves. He invited us to have a seat at the kitchen table. Lionel sat backwards in his chair in an effort to act casual.

"Intrepids hold no ill intention toward the Connoisseurs," he assured us. "The Malamute's club is far too insignificant to concern The Nexus. We're international, with branches in every metropolis from London to Hong Kong. We maintain training facilities near vaunted institutes of higher education from Boston to Austin. The Nexus is a jumbo jet, and the Connoisseurs are a mosquito."

"You don't have what they have, though," J.R. said.

"You mean Secret Pizza? And its psychedelic properties?" Lionel asked. "The Nexus has something better. Something we created in our own labs. Who needs Secret Pizza when we have Dynamic Dust?"

Lionel pressed a buzzer under the table. A stone-faced sophomore in a white lab coat carried in two plates. She set one in front of me and the other in front of J.R. Each plate had a sloppily constructed pizza bagel made with American cheese and store-bought spaghetti sauce. Lionel offered us each one hundred dollars to take one bite.

I went for it. J.R. refused the money but took a bite anyway. I spit the chewy, messy, ill-tasting mess into my napkin and handed back the cash.

"I can't eat that," I declared. "Awful."

Lionel produced a canister of Dynamic Dust. He sprinkled some on the rest of my pizza bagel.

"Try again for two hundred dollars?" he dared me

I refused.

"Five hundred dollars?"

I took another bite. Something was different. Dynamic Dust made the pizza bagel edible. The taste no longer bothered me. In fact, nothing bothered me. I felt pleasantly numb. J.R refused to try Dynamic Dust, even when Lionel upped the offer to one thousand dollars.

"Dynamic Dust turns even a poorly made pizza bagel into a consumable meal," Lionel explained. "Dynamic Dust keeps costs low by utilizing less-desirable and, therefore, more affordable ingredients. As a bonus, it cuts down on food waste. Overcooked? Burnt beyond recognition? No matter. It all tastes the same with a sprinkle of Dynamic Dust. It makes Nexus brand pizzas reliably adequate and globally recognizable."

As a parting gift, Lionel handed us a glossy packet highlighting The Nexus' humanitarian efforts.

J.R. walked me back to his dorm room, where his brother was bunking for the weekend. Mike Grappler, a pre-med student, fed me Ramen noodles and Gloam Pop to counteract the anesthetic effects of Dynamic Dust. The nourishment helped me regain my wits.

As Mike borrowed his brother's shower sandals and toiletry bag, he found a yellow Post-it note stuck to J.R.'s shampoo bottle. The note was decorated with a pizza sketch and a rhyme.

TEST OF STRENGTH
WORTHY OF COACH GABLE
YANK THE PIZZA CUTTER
FROM SAM'S STONE TABLE

"Our challenge takes place at Sam's Pizza," Mike celebrated. "Calzone reload!"

13

EVAN'S DILEMMA AND ANNA'S CLUE

E van spent the day with Anna in her dorm room, where Anna introduced her boyfriend to a Minnesota rock band called Semisonic.

"*Great Divide* is the album title," Anna explained. "Cities 97 radio plays a whole bunch of Semisonic tunes."

Evan slow danced with Anna and gazed around her room. The walls were plastered with posters featuring a popular tennis hunk.

"Could you tell me again why you have so many Andre Agassi posters?" Evan ed.

"Because he's super-duper hot!" Anna asserted. "I'd drop you like a hot potato if I thought I had a shot with Andre Agassi."

Evan pretended to pout in a cutesy way.

"Remind me, who's the guy with all the *Sports Illustrated* swimsuit issues on his nightstand?" Anna teased. "You'd leave me in the dust for Tyra Banks."

"No way," Evan smirked. "Well, maybe for Tyra..."

Anna giggled. They kissed until the loud dorm telephone rang.

BRRRRRRRRRRRIIIIINNNGGGGG!!

BRRRRRRRRRRRIIIIINNNGGGGG!!

Anna untangled herself from Evan's embrace in time to bound over and answer the phone.

"Hello? Oh, Professor Carson! How are ya?"

Anna's effervescent tone dipped an octave after she was informed of the reason for the call.

"I understand. Thank you for calling, Professor. Buh-bye."

Evan braced himself for unhappy news, but Anna was calm and matter-of-fact.

"The UFO I spotted isn't extraterrestrial. It's a man-made satellite."

"A satellite? Like for television?"

"Indeterminate," Anna said. "We'll gather more data tonight."

"Another night at the observatory? I was hoping we could hang out."

"I'm sorry, Ev. I want to spend time with you, believe me. But I should really learn to distinguish between TV satellites and asteroids. For my own future and for the good of mankind."

Evan shifted out of needy boyfriend mode into supportive boyfriend mode. He rubbed Anna's shoulders to demonstrate that he understood her predicament.

"Thank you for always being there for me," she said. "Even though I won't be winning any awards for my discovery."

"You did win one award," Evan said. "They just announced it."

"Oh, really? Which award is that?"

"The Hot Lips Award for hottest lips in the universe."

Anna snickered and kissed her silly boyfriend. She packed her book bag and headed off to Van Allen Hall.

***

Evan returned to our room at Burge and called home to check in with his parents. He got the answering machine at the house, so he tried the store.

"Fromager Records," his sister answered.

"Jen? What are you doing in Naperville?"

"Decided to swing home for a weekend," she said. "Hanging with Mom and Dad, getting some laundry done…"

"Cool. When is Illini Spring Break?"

"Third week of March. We're doing South Padre Island!" Jen exclaimed.

Evan told Jen about his plan to surprise Anna with a trip to Indianapolis. The Bulls would be in Indy to play the Pacers, and Evan wanted to take Anna to a game. Jen advised him to reconsider.

"Indiana in March for a basketball game? Every girl's dream. Take Anna somewhere warm, little brother."

Evan realized it sounded like a selfish vacation, but Anna liked watching Bulls games with him. He reassured himself about the plan as Jen moved on to breaking family news.

"Mom and Dad are cutting bait. They're closing Fromager Records for good. Liquidation begins next week. I'm so sorry, little brother. I know how much this place means to you."

Evan finished catching up with his sister before putting on his designated "sad day" album, Nirvana's *MTV Unplugged in New York*. Kurt Cobain sang "The Man Who Sold The World" (lyrics by David Bowie, according to Theo). The haunting chorus caused Evan to ponder his place as a pawn in a system controlled by monstrosities like the Phantom Wonderstore. Evan decided he needed to fight for his family's legacy. He grabbed his car keys and set course for Naperville.

***

At Van Allen Observatory, Professor Carson presented Anna with a cornbread muffin.

"In Iowa, we don't say 'congratulations,' we say 'corn-gratulations'!"

"Wowzers, it's still warm! Thank you, Professor! Do Iowans really say 'corn-gratulations'?"

"Well, no..." Professor Carson considered. "Only I say that. Perhaps that's why none of my students have ever invited me to a graduation party."

Anna laughed, but not with her typical Minnesota giddiness. Professor Carson tried to lift her spirits.

"I know you were hoping your discovery would turn out to be something from deep space, but the fact it's man-made doesn't diminish your accomplishment. You spotted something that no other astronomer did. That's significant and deserves recognition. Not only that, it requires the attention of the scientific community; to ascertain how that satellite entered our airspace, who put it there, and for what purpose. Privacy and safety are at stake. You've done a service to your fellow citizens, Astronomer Anna Sauser. I salute you and award you...this muffin."

Anna took a bite of the cornbread treat.

"By the way, someone left you a note at the front desk," Professor Carson said.

He handed her a yellow Post-it note with a drawing of a pizza. Teacher and student read the riddle together:

> A MILKY WAY PIZZA
> WITH TOPPINGS SO STARRY
> THIS GLOBULAR CLUSTER
> IS CALLED...

"Omega Centauri!" Professor Carson blurted out. "Sorry, a teacher isn't supposed to shout out the answers."

"No apology necessary," Anna smiled. "Omega Centauri...Discovered by Ptolemy?"

"I'm glad someone's been paying attention to my lectures! Ptolemy discovered Omega Centauri in 150 AD. It was rediscovered by Johann Bayer in 1603 and rediscovered again in 1677 by Edmond Halley, before his famous comet."

"How can one rediscover a thing that's already been discovered?" Anna asked.

"If I could answer that," Professor Carson paused. "I'd be teaching philosophy."

14

QUIZZICAL CHALLENGE

M icky's was packed with students hoping to claim the grand prize of Spring Break airfare for two to any destination in the continental United States. Trivia Trixie sipped ice water at the bar. The contest proctor was a comedian of local acclaim named Cheez Louise. She tapped the mic.

"Final question," Cheez Louise announced. "Which Oscar nominee got her major motion picture start as Mookie's girlfriend in *Do The Right Thing*?"

Trivia Trixie wrote `Rosie Perez` and darted to the front to hand in her answer sheet.

"Where's the fire, freshman?" Cheez Louise joked. "There's no prize for being first. No take backs once you hand in your answer sheet."

Trivia Trixie didn't flinch. She slipped her answer sheet into the designated slot and returned to her seat without glancing at Cheez Louise.

"There goes Little Miss Can't Be Wrong," Cheez Louise mocked, earning chuckles from the crowd.

Micky's staff collected answer sheets and requested time to tally up the final scores. Cheez Louise filled the gap with schtick.

"Speaking of the Oscars, Academy Award nominees were announced. Anyone see *Fargo*? Clap if you saw *Fargo*."

Light applause.

"A few people," Cheez Louise nodded. "Boy, that's one way to use a wood-chipper, eh? And then there's that *Sling Blade* guy with the lawn mower machete. Where do these maniacs shop? Builders Square?"

Minimal laughter.

"That I'd like to see, Slide Blade asking for help at Builders Square," Cheez Louise set herself up for an impression. "Mmmph, reckon you sell Garden Weasels here, mmm-hmm."

Decent laughter.

"Yes sir, Mr. Blade. Right next to the Chia Pets."

More laughter.

"Chia Pets, another thing I don't get," Cheez Louise continued. "'Makes a great gift,' the ad claims. For whom, exactly? People who feel plants aren't lovable enough, but aren't quite ready for the massive responsibility that comes with adopting a hamster, I guess."

Solid laughs.

A Micky's employee handed Cheez Louise a scorecard.

"The results are in, and we have a tie between our defending champ and a newcomer. Raise your hand, Trivia Trixie!"

Trivia Trixie waved at Cheez Louise.

"What do you know? Little Miss Can't Be Wrong actually wasn't wrong. She earned a perfect score. Congrats, freshman!" Cheez Louise acknowledged.

The crowd gave Trixie a round of applause.

"Our reigning champ was also perfect. Step forward, Tommy Anchors!" Cheez Louise announced.

The crowd parted to make way for the formally-dressed, middle-aged man with a chiseled jawline and salt and pepper hair. Tommy Anchors adjusted his tie and shook the hand of Cheez Louise.

"Goes to show what can be accomplished when one has no goals or interests outside of bar trivia," Tommy Anchors joked at his own expense.

Trivia Trixie sensed that Tommy's response reflected genuine humility. She recognized his name from the *Connoisseurs' Compendium.* Tommy Anchors was a Pizza Steward Emeritus.

Cheez Louise quieted the crowd and dramatized the moment.

"As defending champ, Tommy Anchors may choose to answer our tie-break-er or defer to Trivia Trixie."

Tommy Anchors made brief eye contact with his opponent before answering.

"Since it's Trivia Trixie's first Micky's competition, let's test her moxie. I defer."

The crowd "oohed" and "aahed" as Cheez Louise egged them on.

"Tommy Anchors defers to Trivia Trixie! Let's see what she's made of, folks. Trivia Trixie, here is your question, for all the marbles. On the popular sitcom *Friends*, how many sisters does Joey Tribbiani have?

Tommy Anchors' body language indicated he was stumped. Trivia Trixie marched forward and grabbed Cheez Louise's microphone.

"Dina, Gina, Tina, Veronica, Mary Angela, Mary Therese, and Cookie. Seven Tribbiani sisters total."

Trivia Trixie handed the mic back to a stunned Cheez Louise, who mumbled, "'Seven' is correct."

Cheez Louise hesitated to hand over the airline ticket vouchers, so Trivia Trixie snatched them from the comedian's grip. Tommy Anchors congratulated the victor.

"Naming all seven sisters is beyond impressive," he genuflected.

Tommy Anchors handed her a yellow Post-it note. "You earned this clue. Good luck in your venture."

Trivia Trixie thanked him and threw on her coat. She read the three-word clue as she exited Micky's:

CORNY EQUINE SIDEKICK

A Gumby's Pizza delivery vehicle drove down Dubuque Street and honked at Trivia Trixie. The driver nodded as he passed. Trivia Trixie appreciated the coordination of her Connoisseur overseers. The answer to her riddle was clear.

"Gumby's sidekick is a horse named 'Pokey,'" she said to herself. "Too easy."

15

GOOD VIBRATIONS

A sunflower-sized pizza cutter was cemented into the stone table at Sam's Pizza. Mike and J.R. had taken turns yanking the oversized utensil for a solid hour, with zero success, before they decided to take a calzone break and refuel. Mike Grappler groused about the feat of strength he and his brother were issued. He wished for a more scientific challenge. J.R. Grappler dismissed his brother's complaint.

"This *is* science, Michael. Everything is science."

"Sure, if you want to get all technical. But I crave advanced science. Wallace Carothers lab nerd stuff. Not the banality of Newton's laws of motion."

"Remind me, what did Wallace Carothers invent? Spandex?" J.R. asked.

"Nylon," Mike corrected. "Joseph Shivers invented Spandex."

"Good thing he did, or we'd be wrestling in polyester singlets," J.R. said. "That gives me an idea: I should listen to my pre-match mixtape. Remember how Rage Against the Machine got me so hyped I pinned that undefeated heavyweight from Munster?"

"Music brings out the best in you," Mike agreed. "Might help you dislodge that cutter."

A gray-haired gentleman in a black and gold sport coat had been watching the Grappler Twins with great interest. He rose from his chair and entered the conversation.

"Music is also science," he said.

J.R. recognized the man as the most famous opera singer ever to hail from the state of Iowa.

"You're...you're..." J.R. stammered. "It's an honor, sir."

"Call me Simon."

"A thrill to make your acquaintance, Simon," Mike said. "Want to give this pizza cutter a try? Darn thing won't budge."

"Wiggle room starts with vibration," Simon said.

Simon inhaled deeply, then unleashed a powerful bass-baritone vocal note. The pizza cutter started vibrating. The Grappler Twins jiggled the handle, and the cutter loosened. They pushed and pulled until the pizza cutter slid out and dropped to the ground. Simon's vocals faded, but the beauty of the musical note hung in the air. It left nearby diners awestruck. J.R. retrieved a yellow Post-it note off the previously buried end of the pizza cutter.

"Think you could teach me to sing like that, Simon?" Mike asked.

"Honestly? No."

The Grappler Twins shared a laugh with Simon and thanked him for his assistance.

***

Back at Bo-James Bar, The Malamute and Clownfoot hoisted pints of beer to toast the recruitment of worthy successors.

"Not a moment too soon," The Malamute sipped his lager. "Carrying the Secret Pizza torch these past four years has been demanding."

"Time for us to leave college life behind," Clownfoot said. "And get jobs."

The roommates shuddered at the thought of joining the real world.

"You served honorably as Secret Pizza Steward, Malamute."

"And you, Clownfoot, were the most loyal Secret Pizza Chief Connoisseur this campus has ever seen. But perhaps we shouldn't celebrate yet. Evan's team hasn't officially replaced us."

Clownfoot glanced at his watch and surmised that the new Connoisseurs were likely almost done with their individual challenges.

"Hope they fare better than You-Know-Who," Clownfoot said.

"Wily Gene wasn't one of us," The Malamute sighed. "He had us fooled."

"That budlacker lived next door to us in the dorms, Malamute! He didn't even know how to fold a New York slice. He thought deep dish was a late-night gossip show on the E! Network."

The Malamute nodded.

"A pizza rookie, sure. But there's no way we could've predicted he would morph into the pizza supervillain he's become."

"Wily Gene stands as the single biggest threat to the very existence of Secret Pizza," Clownfoot declared. "We must inform Evan and his squad who they're up against. Tonight. After they've gathered the clues. They deserve to be warned."

16

— · —

A STEWARD SAVES HIS FAMILY

A nna took a break from the observatory and stopped at Burge in search of Evan. Instead, she found me alone in the dorm room.

"I thought Evan was with you," I said.

The phone rang.

BRRRRRRRRRRRIIIINNNGGGGG!!

"Hello? What's up, Evan," I said into the phone. "I borrowed your deodorant stick. Hope that's cool. Must've left my Right Guard spray in the shower room..."

Anna confiscated the phone from me.

"Hey, Ev! Where are you?"

Evan was calling from Iowa 80, the World's Largest Truck Stop. He was on his way home to Naperville to prevent his parents from selling the store.

"It finally dawned on me how to save the family business: posters!" Evan exclaimed. "If we can attract customers by selling cool posters, we can take a huge chunk of business from the Phantom Wonderstore!"

Anna noticed her boyfriend sounded frenetic as he rambled on about his last-ditch plan to save Fromager Records. Anna knew Evan was being irrational but understood his emotional state.

"Family first," she said. "I've got Crust here, and we'll handle the whole Secret Pizza thingy. You do what you need to do, babe."

"Thanks, Anna," Evan said. "I love you."

"Love you, too. Crust wants the phone back. Here he is."

I wasn't much for coming up with advice on my own. But I had a good memory for repurposing advice I'd received from others. One such gem popped into my head, and it applied to Evan's predicament.

"Hey," I said. "Bummer about Fromager Records."

"Thanks, Crust."

"I told you about the day I got fired from Contadino's. It crushed me, man. But I'll never forget what my dad's girlfriend, LaTonya, said..."

"Hey, Crust, is this a long story? Because I'm on a payphone, and I only have one more quarter."

"No, it's real quick. I was holding back tears as LaTonya walked me to the parking lot. She told me, 'Beginnings can be uncertain, and endings are often sour. The middle is the good part. Hold the middle memories, not the start or finish.'"

Evan was silent on the other end of the phone, and I got worried.

"Are you mad I used your deodorant?"

"No, Crust," Evan laughed. "All good. I'll be back on Monday. Go Hawkeyes."

I hung up the phone and paced back and forth. I doubted our ability to complete the mission without our team captain. Anna grabbed two Gloam Pops from the mini-fridge and handed one to me.

"Chillax, Crust. Evan needs time to process."

I took a deep breath and opened my can of pop. Anna took a swig of hers.

"Oh heck! That's sugary," she hiccuped. "But tasty, Crust. My compliments."

17

THE CEDAR RAPIDS PRANKSTER

Henry "Hank" Nile Feller was born two months ahead of schedule to Nancy and Gerald Feller of Cedar Rapids. Hank weighed less than three pounds at birth but gained mass at a pace deemed acceptable by the wonderful doctors at St. Luke's. Gerald and Nancy brought the tiny bundle of bliss home to meet his older brothers and sisters after a few weeks of incubation.

Feller Farms, once a fully operational corn supplier, transformed into an entertainment venue in the mid-1970s. A billboard on the main road enticed drivers with the promise of Iowa's Largest Corn Maze. The labyrinth wound through twenty-five acres of live corn, past the Feller Farms Petting Zoo, the Feller Farms Pony Rides, the Feller Farms Cow Milking Experience, the Feller Farms Rascally Rabbits Show, the Feller Farms Chick Hatching Room, and the Feller Farms Gift Shop. Visitors arrived from as far away as Maine.

October was the busiest month as Feller Farms shifted into Halloween mode. Feller Frights Haunted Maze delighted and frightened the greater Cedar Rapids community each autumn with an evolving array of scares and surprises. The Feller children dressed as ghouls and goblins, made rubber vampire bats fly, and used machinery to animate scarecrows. Hank was four when his older sister Sandra first painted his face to look like a demon child. Little Hank emerged from the corn and stared down thrill-seekers. Demon Hank's appearance averaged three blood-curdling screams per evening. His older brothers and sisters praised his performance.

Gerald ran the family business while Nancy worked sales for a cereal company. Boxes with cartoon mascots packed the Feller cupboard. The mascots could hardly contain their excitement about marshmallows, or chocolate, or marshmallows *and* chocolate. Hank shared their enthusiasm, especially when the mascots promised a toy inside the box. One box of marshmallow goodness presented Hank with a sticky wall crawler. He asked Gerald to explain how it worked, and Gerald pointed to the instructions on the back of the cereal box. Hank stared at where his father pointed, but Gerald noted a lack of comprehension.

"Can you see how the girl on the box plays with the toy, son?"

Hank wrinkled his nose.

Gerald and Nancy took five-year-old Hank to a specialist, who diagnosed the child with a vision disorder. Eye drops and injections became a regular part of Hank's routine, and his vision improved tenfold. The world became far more vibrant.

Hank overheard parental conversations and knew there was a chance he'd suffer vision loss again. Desperate to store sights forever in his memory, Hank spent many hours looking at photos of his family, then closing his eyes and trying to envision their faces. It worried him that he couldn't always come up with a clear picture of a face. His four older siblings tended to mash together in his mind's eye.

Hank played with the wall crawler long after it had lost a degree of stickiness and became caked with dust, bug particles, and grime. One mundane morning he threw the sticky wall crawler against the wall while he brushed his teeth before school. An urgent knock at the door hurried Hank out of the kids' bathroom so Sandra could do her hair. As the youngest, Hank was used to limited bathroom time, so he exited without a fuss. Sandra shut the door. Seconds later, Hank heard Sandra shriek. She ran out of the bathroom with the wall crawler stuck in her hair.

"Tarantula!" Sandra screamed. "Get it out! Get it out!"

Hank's oldest brother, Phil, untangled the sticky wall crawler and showed it to Sandra. She recognized the item and glowered at Hank before returning to the bathroom with an emphatic door slam. Phil giggled and handed the sticky wall crawler back to his littlest brother.

After school that day, Hank did his private memory exercises with family photos. Sandra stood out. The expression on her face after that creepy crawler landed in her hair seared itself into Hank's brain.

Phil took Hank downtown to George Tumble's Magic Shop to buy a whoopee cushion, fake vomit, and trick chewing gum. Prankster Hank found his calling. Phil showed him how to inflate the whoopee cushion. They planted it under their brother Jeff's seat at the dinner table.

PRRRRRRRRRRRABBBBBBPPPPPPPPPTTTTTTT!!!

Even Gerald giggled at the loud gaseous noise when Jeff sat down.

The next day, Hank closed his eyes and pictured Jeff's red cheeks and astonished chuckle.

On school picture day, Hank pranked his sister Dolly with gum that turned her teeth black. She chased her little brother around the breakfast table until Phil assured Dolly the stain was temporary. She rushed upstairs to rinse her mouth. Dolly's death stare was imprinted in Hank's memory.

Phil's caddy money funded Hank's gags. When Phil left for college, Hank spent his allowance at the joke shop.

One day, Gerald Feller walked out to feed the chickens and caught twelve-year-old Hank smoking a cigarette.

"Need a smoke?" adolescent Prankster Hank deadpanned, as if they were barroom pals.

In disbelief, Gerald snatched the cigarette from the boy's lips. It turned out to be a phony cigarette from the joke shop. Gerald stormed off, unsure of how angry to be at his son. Hank couldn't wait to tell Phil about the successful prank.

Phil was due home from Lawrence, Kansas, for Thanksgiving. He never made it. On his way back from school, Phil was killed in a car accident. The Feller family was shattered.

Instead of saying a prayer at the wake, Hank whispered to Phil through the closed casket. He described the befuddled face their dad made as he examined the bogus cigarette. At the post-funeral reception, a spider scurried across surly

Uncle Vern's potato salad and almost gave the old grump a conniption. Hank was certain the spider was sent by Phil.

Hank worried he wouldn't be able to picture Phil's face, but his concerns were unfounded. He closed his eyes and saw Phil in hysterics, laughing at the whoopee cushion, the gum gag, and the sticky wall crawler in Sandra's hair.

The telephone was a terrific source of amusement for early teenage Prankster Hank. Dolly participated in Hank's phony radio station giveaway gag. Prankster Hank called random numbers and informed whomever answered they'd won a grand prize. Then Hank would hand the phone over to his "station manager," played by Dolly, who told the poor folks the whole thing had been a mistake, and they were not the winners. Unfortunately for Hank and Dolly, a new service of the phone company allowed a call recipient to return a call by dialing *69. Hank's father answered the return call, and the whole radio station prank unraveled. Gerald was embarrassed by his son and daughter's antics, but instead of confronting Hank and Dolly, he decided to teach them a lesson.

A week later, Gerald surprised Hank and Dolly with a stop at Wilbur's Bike Shop, where they each picked out a brand new mountain bike. Gerald paid for the bikes and loaded them in the family truck. Hank and Dolly were discussing which trails they wanted to ride when Gerald made a sudden detour. He pulled up to an unknown address and walked the kids up to the front door. A woman answered, and Gerald introduced himself.

"I'm Gerald Feller. We spoke on the phone. And these are my two phony prize barons. They've brought a present for each one of your kids. Go unload the bicycles, Hank and Dolly."

If Hank had been in front of a mirror, he would've remembered the look on his own face. He certainly noted Dolly's dismay.

"Go on, now, Mr. Radio DJ," Gerald said. "You promised a prize giveaway. Time to pay the piper."

Hank and Dolly trudged to the truck and wheeled the bikes onto the driveway. Two jubilant youngsters ran out of the house to accept the gifts. On the ride home, Gerald informed Hank and Dolly the bicycle money would be deducted from their allowances. Paying for the bikes stung, but Hank found consolation in the joy of giving.

Nancy Feller hosted a book club with her friends. Pizza carryout from Leonardo's was a staple of the Cedar Readers monthly meetings. Hank munched on cheese pizza while listening to the ladies express empathy for the soldiers of *The Things They Carried* or highlight Biblical correlations alluded to in *A Prayer for Owen Meany*. Hank had been a bookworm ever since he learned to read. His literary appetite accelerated around the same time his vision problem was diagnosed, and he advanced from *Clifford the Big Red Dog* to *Beezus and Ramona* almost overnight. Hank felt he was in a race against time.

Should I ever go blind, I want to have already read every book in the library so I won't feel left out.

A doctor's appointment in his freshman year of high school confirmed Hank's retinas were stronger than ever and that vision problems would no longer haunt him. He prayed to Phil, requesting occasional reminders to be thankful for the gift of clear sight.

Prankster Hank made friends with ease. Friendship was a bond he took seriously. Pulling a prank on a friend was Hank's way of showing love. Hijinks were in his blood. Hank matured into a Halloween mastermind at Feller Farms. Headless horsemen, zombie chickens, and flatulent Frankenstein monsters were a few of his greatest hits.

***

February 8, 1997, Four O'Clock In The Afternoon. Eight Hours Until National Pizza Day

Prankster Hank spent Saturday afternoon at The Airliner re-reading his favorite book, *The Wind in the Willows*. He turned to page 100 and found a yellow Post-it note with a pizza sketch and a rhyme:

PULL A RIVALRY PRANK

ON A GOLDEN GOPHERS FAN

PROVE YOUR LOVE OF PIZZA

IS NO FLASH IN THE PAN

The practical joke center of Prankster Hank's brain started churning. He located Cloris the waitress and whispered in her ear. At Hank's request, Cloris approached a table where two University of Minnesota students were awaiting a pizza order. Cloris was a Des Moines native and a lifelong Hawkeyes fan, so rivalry with the Golden Gophers came naturally.

"We're running a special promotion today for out-of-state visitors," Cloris mentioned. "Sing a karaoke song, and your pizza is on the house!"

As Cloris anticipated, the Gopher fans were hesitant.

"Nobody wants to hear us clumsy galoots sing. Trust me," the nice guy in the maroon shirt said.

"Oh, come on," Cloris insisted. "You'll be grand! Earlier today, a Minnesota fan performed "Purple Rain," and it was fabulous."

The even nicer guy, who sported a Golden Gophers hat, fell into Cloris' trap.

"Now, a Prince song—that's a whole different story. All us Minnesotans can sing along to Prince songs. Almost can't help ourselves when a Prince song starts playing."

"Now you're talking!" Cloris sealed the deal. "I'll have the DJ queue one up!"

Cloris raced over and whispered in the ear of the DJ, who welcomed the Golden Gophers fans to the stage. The Airliner dining room showered the visitors with boos.

"Geez, tough crowd," the nice guy smiled.

"Guess we're really doing this, eh?" the nicer guy smiled even wider.

The DJ spun his turntable, and the music began—only it wasn't a song by Minnesota's most treasured resident, but rather a tune called "Two Princes" by Spin Doctors.

"Hold on a tick," the nice guy pleaded. "This isn't Prince!"

"Ope, my bad!" Cloris winked. "You said 'prince song,' and this is a song about princes."

"She's got us on a technicality," the nicer guy shrugged.

"Don't get shy on me now, Minnesota Men!" Cloris encouraged. "You gotta earn your pizza around these parts!"

The Minnesotans bobbed their heads to the pop song and read the lyrics from the karaoke screen. Soon the entire restaurant was cheering them on. The Golden Gopher crooners rode the crowd's enthusiasm and belted out the lyrics, giving it all they had. The Airliner rocked out to Spin Doctors, led by a pair of genial out-of-towners. From his stool, Prankster Hank beamed as the practical joke played out to perfection. Cloris breezed by and gave him a high-five.

"Not bad for a pair of Golden Gophers," Prankster Hank chair-danced. "Put their pizza on my tab."

"Already did, Hankster," Cloris said, before handing him the clue he earned.

Prankster Hank rushed his clue back to Burge, where he handed it over to Anna.

HITCHHIKER FROM THE NORTH STAR STATE WHOSE DIA-
MOND WISH CAME TRUE

"I'm lousy at solving these," Hank admitted. "Any thoughts, Anna? You're from Minnesota."

Anna realized the answer was a movie character her dad frequently referenced, Moonlight Graham from *Field of Dreams*.

"We oughta pin up all the clues like Mulder does on *The X-Files*," Anna figured.

Anna pulled Evan's poster board off the wall and removed the magazine cutouts of Tyra Banks.

"We'll need all five clues to get the full picture," Anna decided. "Let's gather the team at the library."

18

SNOW-COVERED GIL

C hill Gil wandered into Falbo Bros. for a slice of cheese pizza. He set his tray on a table while he filled his fountain drink. When he returned to sit down, Chill Gil noticed a yellow Post-it note attached to the tray. It had the following message:

> YOU'RE ADEPT AT GAMES
> LIKE DARTS AND POOL
> FACE A JENGA MASTER
> AND KEEP YOUR COOL

He looked up at the front window. Taped to the glass was a flier promoting the Giant Jenga Contest at Sports Column. Gil finished his slice, then headed home to put on his lucky jersey.

***

Betsy Steenbock was a member of the Green Bay Sideliners, a professional dance team associated with the Packers. Hence, Betsy's son, Gil, had the opportunity to be a ballboy at Green Bay Packers training camp. The bespectacled kid's laid-back, philosophical demeanor amused the football players. Star wideout

Sterling Sharpe bestowed a nickname when he autographed a game-worn jersey
for the youngster.

```
To my main man, Chill Gil,
Go Pack Go!
Sterling Sharpe
```

When the Sideliners disbanded in the late 1980s, Betsy accepted a beer dis-
tributor job. She and Gil moved to Monroe, Wisconsin.

Betsy's hobby was cross-country skiing. Gil inherited his mom's appreciation
for the leisure activity. Betsy taught Gil how to bend his hips and glide over the
snow. Gil found splendor in the serenity of the unbroken snow, the rhythmic
whoosh of his snow pants, and the cold air in his lungs.

Betsy did business with a tavern called Yountie's, and it was Gil's favorite
lunch spot. Mother and son could leave their skis in the rack out front and stop
in for a three-cheese pizza featuring Wisconsin cheddar, Wisconsin mozzarella,
and Wisconsin asiago. The gooey warmth of Yountie's cheesy slices unfroze Gil's
cheeks. Yountie's staff was friendly, and the service was exquisite. Betsy and Gil
threw darts or played pool while they digested.

Betsy had a knack for client relations and consumer trends. She butted heads
with her supervisor, a hard-headed buffoon who was short on strategy. Around
the Steenbock home, Betsy's boss was known as "Dunce Lombardi." Dunce
wanted to push Yountie's beer coast-to-coast and make it a national brand. Betsy
believed the value was in keeping the beer exclusive to Wisconsin. She advised
the Yountie family to stay local. The client agreed and ignored Dunce's overture.
Dunce accused Betsy of sabotage. Eventually, Betsy tired of Dunce's nonsense
and convinced Yountie's to hire her as brand manager.

As a teen, Chill Gil felt compelled to live up to his nickname. For that reason,
he hid his emotional issues. Gil struggled with anxiety attacks, but he didn't
want to bother his hardworking mother.

His junior year, Gil volunteered to man a booth at Ameche High School's
Dairy Days Festival. Organizers stationed Gil at the milk bottle toss, where

contestants who knocked over all six bottles could win a stuffed cow. Gil's hands trembled as he attempted to stack the bottles. A line of contestants waited impatiently. Gil abandoned his post and left the festival.

A school counselor recommended therapy. Gil hated the idea of telling some stranger his problems, but Betsy begged him to give it one honest chance. Gil wore his Sterling Sharpe jersey to the first session with Dr. Melinda Herber. Melinda complimented Gil's jersey while expressing sympathy for Sterling Sharpe, who had recently retired due to a neck injury.

"Sterling will come back. I don't believe his retirement is final," Gil asserted.

"Why are you so certain Sharpe will return?" Melinda wondered. "He announced his retirement. Seemed definitive about his decision."

"Because he's unstoppable. He's Sterling Sharpe."

"What if he *wanted* to stop? For his own well-being?" Melinda asked. "Would you lose respect for him? Would he no longer be cool?"

Gil thought before answering.

"Sterling Sharpe will be cool no matter what," Gil finally said.

"If your hero can take his foot off the pedal, would it also be acceptable for you, Gil, to address your own health and well-being?"

Gil understood Melinda's intent.

"Sure," he nodded. "If Sterling can give up the game he loves, I can do a little therapy."

Gil reported to Melinda's office weekly for chats about Packers football. Gil opened up about his insecurities as well. He referenced his mom's resolve.

"I wish I inherited her strength. I'm probably like my dad, whoever he is."

Melinda disagreed.

"You are Gil," she said. "Not some carbon copy of a DNA strand. Your experiences have shaped you. Your mom's determination rubbed off on you more than you realize."

Melinda repeated the mantra in her subsequent sessions with Gil. Gil began to notice ways he took after his mom. The more he started to feel like Betsy Steenbock's son, the less anxious Gil felt. His anxiety attacks subsided.

At the end of senior year, Gil was worried about concluding his therapy with Melinda and moving to Iowa City. Melinda gave him a tactic he could use to fend off anxious feelings. Any time he felt overwhelmed, Gil closed his eyes and imagined himself cross-country skiing through a snowy field. He listened for the whoosh of his snow pants and breathed cold air into his lungs. He pictured his mom up ahead of him, leading the way.

***

Moments before Chill Gil entered Sports Column on that February night in 1997, he used Melinda's method to calm his nerves. He felt at ease when the gamerunner called his name as Jenga Jim's first challenger of the night. Chill Gil glided up to the stacking circle.

Jenga Jim stood six foot seven and weighed in excess of three hundred pounds. Giant Jenga was the college senior's forte. Jenga Jim hadn't lost a match since March of 1994, after a Garth Brooks concert at Carver-Hawkeye Arena, when one of Garth's roadies bested the then-freshman stacking sensation.

Jenga Jim wore a cowboy hat, but never indoors. He removed his hat before he walked through the front door of Sports Column and placed it atop the coat rack. Garth Brooks' "Standing Outside the Fire" blared from the jukebox. Jenga Jim was well-manicured for a farm kid and dressed with more flash than his hometown buddies. The bedazzled "Jenga Jim" leather vest was a birthday gift from his girlfriend, Cloris.

Chill Gil was polishing his glasses with the Sterling Sharpe jersey when a shadow cast over him. Jenga Jim held out a gargantuan paw, and Chill Gil shook his hand.

"Howdy," Jenga Jim said. "Ready to stack?"

As the challenger, it was Chill Gil's responsibility to build the Jenga tower. His stack was tight, and Jenga Jim gave it the thumbs up after a quick inspection. The stacker, Chill Gil, moved first.

As the tower climbed higher, Jenga Jim's height became an advantage. Chill Gil's strategy turned aggressive. He tapped a foundational block out of the third row from bottom and stacked it on the higher side of the pinnacle. Jenga Jim stabilized the tower with a balancing counter move, extending the game. Chill Gil doubled-down, selecting another third row block for removal. The tower wobbled but remained upright. Jenga Jim tried another counterbalance move. The attempt failed. The Jenga tower toppled and crashed to the floor. Victory belonged to Chill Gil. Jenga Jim patted him on the back and rewarded him with a yellow Post-it note.

"You earned this clue, partner," Jenga Jim said. "Happy trails."

19

_— • —_

FORTUITOUS PIT STOP

E van sped eastbound on I-88 with his mind fixed on saving Fromager
Records. He was mad at his mom and dad for caving in to the Phan-
tom Wonderstore and all its pomposity. Evan predicted that the allure of the
Wonderstore would wane, and customers would return to the authenticity of
Fromager Records.

Why must my parents be so shortsighted?

It was up to Evan to make Junior and Sally Fromager see the light; their prog
rock son was returning to save the day.

Evan paged through his CD booklet and found a disc his sister had burned
titled _Summer '95_. Evan popped Jen's mix in the hand-me-down Toyota Camry's CD player. Jen's compilation kicked off with "I'll Be There For You," the
Friends TV theme song. The timing struck Evan as uncanny, as he was near the
exit leading to Theo's house in Lake Geneva. Evan reflected on the vow he made
to be a better friend.

He exited the highway in Rochelle, Illinois, and pulled the Camry into the
parking lot of Alfaro's Pizza. Evan wandered inside. The hostess sensed that the
young man was in distress and asked if Evan was alright. He could barely manage
a shrug. The hostess took Evan's coat and fetched him a glass of water. Alfaro's
delivery guy tried to cheer Evan up with a funny story about the time he ran
out of gas during a blizzard. A group of locals sitting at a table by the window
invited Evan to join them. They fixed him a plate with salad, bread, and several
squares of cheese pizza. The woman at the head of the table, Joan, asked about

his troubles. Evan looked up from his plate and broke into tears. He told Joan about Fromager Records. Joan touched Evan's hand and offered him her napkin to dry his tears.

"There's another thing bothering me," Evan confessed. "I was supposed lead my friends on an important mission this weekend. I bailed on them because I was nervous about taking on the challenge."

"We all face self-doubt from time to time," Joan counseled. "You could ask one of your friends to take the lead if you're not comfortable."

"This is going to sound crazy," Evan whispered. "But I have a special ability. I'm the only one who can do the job. It's a lot of pressure."

Joan moved closer to Evan and spoke in a hushed tone.

"Just because you have a gift doesn't mean you're obligated to follow that path. Your destiny is your own, Evan. Follow your heart and do what it's telling you to do."

Something in Joan's inflection caught Evan's attention.

"You have a supertalent, too, don't you?" Evan guessed.

"I can predict where people are headed," Joan smiled. "My family has been running the gas station next door for three generations. Ever since I was a girl, I could envision folks' destinations as soon as they pulled up to the pump. Weird skill, eh?"

"Darn cool, if you ask me," Evan said. "Can you tell where I'm headed?"

"Since the instant you sat down. And I think you know too."

Joan gave Evan a motherly hug. Evan hugged her back. Then he hugged the hostess and the delivery man.

Evan Fromager III walked out of Alfaro's Pizza with a clear mind. Joan met him next door at Bob's Gas and filled Evan's tank.

"Bob is your father?" he asked.

"Grandfather, actually," Joan said. "Bob Fomptelonski."

Evan couldn't believe his ears. Bob Fomptelonski was the made-up name Theo pulled out of thin air to go along with a video game tune. Now, Evan was face-to-face with the granddaughter of a man who went by that very unique name. Before Evan could summon any words or follow-up questions, Joan instructed him to stay put while she ran inside the station. She returned with gifts for him: a roadmap and a package of Blu Tack putty.

"Posters aren't going to save Fromager Records, are they?" Evan asked.

"No, but keep the putty for your dorm walls. Comes in handy," Joan winked.

"Thanks, Joan, but I'm not returning to the dorms tonight. The welcome I experienced at Alfaro's reinforced my belief in the importance of local pizzerias. Every neighborhood deserves an Alfaro's. The Malamute told me about a town where the entire pizza scene was decimated..."

Evan looked at the map. Blandville, Iowa was circled. Joan shrugged like Michael Jordan after he drilled multiple three-pointers in the 1992 NBA Finals.

"My supertalent," Joan smiled.

"Thank you for everything, Joan Fomptelonski," Evan said.

Joan kissed Evan's cheek and wished him good luck. Evan pulled out of Bob's Gas and merged onto I-88 West, back towards Iowa.

20

— • —

PIECING TOGETHER THE CLUES

T rivia Trixie was on shift at the Main Library reference desk, but the crowd was sparse on a Saturday night, leaving Trixie with few official duties. Our group of burgeoning Connoisseurs had the first floor of the library to ourselves. Prankster Hank sat at a table paging through *The House on Mango Street* with one hand while rubbing a balloon on Chill Gil's head with the other, causing Gil's hair to stand up via static electricity. Gil meditated, unbothered by the balloon and possibly even enjoying the scalp sensation. Trixie and Anna pinned clues to the bulletin board. I carried in a tray of cold Gloam Pops, distributed one each to Hank and Gil, and handed a Pie Milkshake to Trivia Trixie.

"You stopped at Hamburg Inn, Crust? That's very thoughtful of you. It's been a boring shift, but this makes it more tolerable. Thank you," Trixie smiled.

Truthfully, it was Anna who suggested the act of kindness. Nonetheless, I was proud of myself for making Trixie happy.

"Let's go over Gil's clue again," Anna said.

A SINGULAR SURNAME HOMOPHONE FOR A FIRST-RATE FIC-
TIONAL POOL PLAYER

"Minnesota Fats is the pool player," Prankster Hank said, glancing up from his book. "From the Walter Tevis novel."

"Of course," Trixie said. "The singular of the surname Fats is Fat. And the homophone..."

"Homophones are words that are pronounced the same but differ in meaning or spelling," Hank, the English major, clarified. "The homophone of Fat is Phat with a *P-H*."

The Grappler Twins hustled in with apologies for tardiness. J.R. despised running late and appeared agitated with his brother. Mike made an unscheduled stop at the bookstore while J.R. finalized a project at the chemistry lab. Mike lost track of time and failed to meet up with J.R. at the agreed-upon hour.

"We were on our way to a *library*, Mike," J.R. chastised him. "Did it occur to you that the university library might have books? And bonus, they're all free."

"Suppose that should've crossed my mind," Mike laughed. "For a straight-A student, I can be rather dense on occasion."

"Same here," Anna admitted. "Total ditz about the simplest things. Yet, plop me in front of a telescope, and I can focus all my brainpower on a celestial thingamabob like nobody's business."

J.R. Grappler dug into his pocket and held up the written clue.

"I hardly broke a sweat removing that giant pizza cutter," Mike joked. "J.R., on the other hand, was drippin' like Scottie Pippen."

J.R. gave his brother a playful shove and handed the clue to Trivia Trixie.

OVERPASS FOR A GOTH DENTIST TURNED FAMOUS FARMER

Prankster Hank said he knew a dentistry major who was into goth culture. The dentistry building was across the river from the library.

"I'm not so sure that's the answer, Hank," Trixie rebutted. "Iowa native Grant Wood asked his dentist to pose as a farmer for his classic painting *American Gothic*. GOTH-ic."

"Trixie with the art smarts!" Anna applauded.

Trixie deflected the praise, instead crediting her Twentieth Century Art T.A.

"Where does the overpass figure in?" I asked, wanting to hear Trixie teach us more.

Trixie held up a finger as if she were about to answer before abruptly running away down an adjoining hallway.

"Ope! And she's off," Anna called like a racetrack announcer.

Chill Gil awoke from his meditation with a location in mind.

"Minnesota is the key. Think about it. You've got Moonlight Graham, who's a doctor from Minnesota. My riddle centered on Minnesota Fats. Seems like the clues are pointing us to the North Star State."

Gil's hypothesis made sense to me. I was eager to embark on the next leg of the journey. J.R. offered to drive. Anna stopped us before we grabbed our coats.

"Hold your horses there, gents. I grew up in Minnesota, and I oughta warn you that our large Scandinavian population means we're famous for our herring."

"So you're saying we should be on the lookout for a seafood restaurant?" I asked.

"No, Crust. I mean herring as in *red* herring," Anna said.

I was confused. Luckily, Trivia Trixie re-entered the room and bailed me out.

"Red herrings are delusive clues meant to throw you off the track," Trixie explained.

Trivia Trixie showed us the book she was carrying, a large tome titled *History of Cedar Rapids, Iowa*.

"Cedar Rapids? That's my hometown," Prankster Hank grinned.

"The dentist who posed for *American Gothic* was also from Cedar Rapids, Hank," Trixie said. "As a thank you to the dentist, Grant Wood gifted him with a painting of a bridge."

Holding the book aloft, Trivia Trixie showed us a picture of the Grant Wood bridge painting.

"The painting has since disappeared," Trixie said. "Even the dentist's children don't know what became of it. It's one of America's great art history mysteries."

"Bridge as in 'overpass,'" I said, putting two-and-two together.

Trivia Trixie turned to the book's atlas and found a map of Cedar Rapids.

"The town has dozens of old bridges," she sighed. "And there's no record of which bridge the painting depicts. Quaker Bridge, Rosedale Bridge, Chiron Bridge..."

Anna unzipped her JanSport book bag and pulled out an astronomy note-book.

"Professor Carson gave a lecture about Chiron," she said, perusing her notes. "Chiron was the wisest and justest of all the centaurs. The ultimate centaur."

"Omega Centauri," Trixie summarized. "Good work, Anna!"

Anna did a funny curtsy, before continuing the story of Chiron.

"A poison arrow pierced Chiron's foot. He attempted to heal himself with herbs, to no avail."

"Been there, Chiron," Prankster Hank joked. "Tried to heal myself with herb on many an occasion."

Hank earned a laugh from the group. Anna allowed the laughter to simmer before she concluded the story of Chiron.

"Upon his death, Chiron was rewarded with an eternal place in the night sky, becoming a constellation."

Trixie called us over to the reference desk and showed us two maps of Cedar Rapids, one new and one old.

"On the modern-day map, crossing over the Chiron Bridge leads to an un-incorporated area," Trixie noted. "But the older map designates a town called Chiron on the far side of the Chiron Bridge."

We had a destination.

I was disheartened to learn that Trixie and Anna wouldn't be accompanying us on the journey to Cedar Rapids. Trixie had to finish her work shift, and Anna was returning to the observatory. She figured there was no sense neglecting her Astronomy Club duties if Evan wasn't participating in the Secret Pizza adventure. I begged the ladies to reconsider.

"You can do this, Crust. You're no nincompoop," Anna said. "Besides, this seems like a fun mission for the boys. Time for you studs to do the heavy lifting."

"Anna's right. We can do this," Prankster Hank flexed his arms. "Just the dudes."

"Don't get lost, boys," Trixie said, handing a roadmap to J.R. Grappler.

***

J.R.'s Ford Expedition sped northbound on I-380. I sat behind Mike Grappler, who was able to outmaneuver Prankster Hank and claim shotgun. Hank settled for the window seat behind the driver, and Chill Gil sat middle back. I cracked a Gloam Pop and bobbed my head to "Wheelz of Steel" until the traveling music was interrupted by a call on J.R.'s car phone. Mike lowered the stereo volume.

"Hello?" J.R. answered. "What's up, Evan? Are you on a payphone?"

J.R. listened for a few seconds and hung up after he said, "Meet you there."

"Keep an eye out for the Blandville exit," J.R. told us.

"Blandville?" I repeated. "Sounds bland."

21

SPACE CAM

Clownfoot and The Malamute sat on the hallway floor outside our dorm room, throwing a Koosh ball back and forth. Anna, who trekked back to Burge to grab her calculator, was tickled to see the familiar twosome playing catch.

"Nice Koosh," she said.

"Astronomer Anna!" Clownfoot exclaimed. "Is Evan with you?"

"Nope. Borrowed Crust's keys so I could retrieve my TI-81. Then it's off to the observatory to record data on a satellite hovering over Iowa."

Clownfoot and The Malamute exchanged a look of alarm and insisted Anna show them the satellite. She agreed to let them use the telescope under her supervision. Clownfoot hopped to his feet and sprinted down the hallway. The Malamute and Anna watched him leave.

"I still need to grab my cal-kee-laytor," Anna said. "Is he running all the way to the observatory?"

"Clownfoot is overstimulated," The Malamute said. "We'll hold the elevator for you."

Anna led them to the observatory, where The Malamute peered through the high-powered telescope. Clownfoot waited impatiently for a turn, tapping his giant foot until The Malamute finally ceded the lens.

"Finally," Clownfoot huffed. "Telescope hog."

"Get a gander at the satellite?" Anna asked.

The Malamute nodded.

"And?"

"It's Wily," he said.

"Definitely Wily," Clownfoot concurred, with one eye glued to the telescope lens.

"Cartoon coyotes are wily," Anna disputed. "This satellite is sophisticated. It features state-of-the-art propulsion and high-powered transponders. Estimated weight is three tons, the size of a rhinoceros."

Clownfoot remained bent over the telescope lens, studying the satellite. Unlike most observatory visitors, who tended to speak in hushed tones befitting the studious lab environment, Clownfoot spoke with such volume that his voice bounced off the walls.

"The Malamute wasn't using 'wily' as an adjective, Astronomer Anna," Clownfoot explained. "The guy who financed this particular satellite goes by the name Wily Gene. He lived next door to us in the dorms freshman year. Wily Gene is the one controlling that hunk of hovering hardware."

"Funding a satellite is no hobby. This fella must have more dough than Oprah Winfrey," Anna remarked.

"He's loaded. Wily Gene inherited family money," Clownfoot confirmed. "Word is he's constructing a huge mansion on Lake Winnibigoshish."

"It's not on Lake Winnibigoshish," The Malamute argued. "It's on Lake Kabetogama."

Clownfoot abandoned the telescope and got in The Malamute's face.

"Winnibigoshish," he stated, "I know this for a fact."

"Take a chill pill, Clownfoot," The Malamute said. "It's Kabetogama."

Clownfoot moved closer, inches from his best friend's face.

"I'm as cool as the other side of the pillow," Clownfoot retorted. "It's Winnibigoshish."

The Malamute recoiled and asked if Clownfoot had been eating sour cream and onion potato chips. Clownfoot breathed into his own hand and smelled it.

"My breath is fine."

"Says you," The Malamute mocked.

Clownfoot put a piece of Winterfresh gum in his mouth.

"I'm done arguing with you," Clownfoot decided. "It's Lake Winnibigoshish. That's that."

Anna had heard enough of the fruitless mansion debate.

"OK. Break it up," she said. "Neutral corners, roomies. Let's focus. Tell me why Wily would launch a satellite into airspace over Iowa."

"Well," The Malamute began. "Wily may have gobs of money..."

"But what he doesn't have," Clownfoot chomped on his gum. "Is the secret behind Secret Pizza."

Anna doubted the veracity of the claim.

"All that trouble to steal a pizza recipe?"

"Of course," Clownfoot said. "That overzealous budlacker needs it to complete his goal of world domination."

Anna did a double-take.

"Shiver me timbers, did you say 'world domination'? I thought this whole Secret Pizza thing was more of a lark. Like a treasure hunt or an adventure club."

The Malamute's tone turned ominous.

"It's far beyond what you imagined, Astronomer Anna. Our crusade is of dire consequence for all mankind."

"Alrighty, then," Anna pulled up a stool. "Start from the beginning. I want to know every detail about this Wily character."

22

---·---

HOW WILY GENE EXPLOITED PIZZA

I n the 1920s, the Clunch family transported illegal Canadian booze for Al Capone via the Great Lakes. They invested the liquor money in land and established themselves as one of the wealthiest families in Wisconsin.

Whitford Clunch, born in 1946, was afforded a life of excess. He developed his love for sailing aboard his family's many boats. He traveled the world, cavorting with women on every continent. Whitford never imagined settling down, as he boasted the open water as his mistress. His perspective changed during a beer-soaked welcome party at the East Lothian Yacht Club in Scotland. A dark-haired debutante named Tyne sassed him. Whitford liked the challenge and returned to the club to try and win her over. Tyne relented and agreed to spend time on his ship, where they found common ground. Whitford brought Tyne to the States, and they were married. The newlyweds purchased the top floor of a Milwaukee high-rise. Marriage was a nonstop party for the first year. Then Tyne got pregnant, which meant she could no longer hop from shindig to shindig on her husband's arm. Whitford grew weary of the inconvenient situation, so he bought Tyne a big house in Lake Geneva. There she could relax while Whitford gallivanted around the globe. Their son was born in 1975. Tyne named the boy Eugene after the famous playwright Eugene O'Neill. She liked the attention of having a baby at first, but the excitement faded before the boy learned to crawl. The tedium of motherhood wore on Tyne. She opted for social activities at the local yacht club and left most of the child-rearing duties to Eugene's nanny, the ebullient Margaret Elster.

Margaret spent an hour per night treating Eugene's frizzy hair. Tyne found the frizz unappealing and required her son's hair to be straightened regularly. Margaret invented fun games to keep Eugene entertained while she combed his hair. Rubber hair ties bothered Eugene, so Margaret styled a flexible band that didn't yank on his scalp. When Margaret read books to Eugene, she did character voices and added her own commentary on flimsy plotlines. Margaret played Pro Kadima with Eugene at the beach and made sure he reapplied sunscreen. When he missed a spot, Margaret rubbed aloe on his sunburnt skin. Margaret nicknamed the boy "Wily" for his commitment to chasing gulls at the edge of the lake, with a success rate on par with Wile E. Coyote.

"Wee Wily Gene," Margaret snickered. "You're a hoot, kiddo."

Margaret came to regret her endorsement of Eugene's bird chasing. One June afternoon, as the lake breeze turned chilly, Margaret decided it was time to head home. She folded the beach chairs and aired out the towels. She picked up an empty cup of yogurt and carried it to the trash receptacle. That was when she heard a terrifying shriek. Margaret turned toward the water and spotted Eugene clutching the wing of a sizable gull. The gull squawked ferociously at the boy, who stood undeterred by the bird's rancor.

"Let him go, Eugene!" Margaret shouted.

Eugene glanced at Margaret, then back at the bird. He jerked its wing down, slamming the gull into the sand. Finally, he released his grip, and the bird flew away over the water. Margaret hurried to Eugene and grabbed him by the shoulders.

"What the heck happened?" Margaret asked. "You shouldn't mess with birds like that."

"He swooped at me," Eugene cried. "It wasn't my fault."

Margaret comforted the boy, and they left the beach without discussing it further. Margaret considered the incident a tremendous failure of her duties as a caretaker.

First I cheer him on about the birds, then I leave him unattended.

Although Margaret chastised herself for lackadaisical nannying, she knew Eugene's behavior was concerning. She reported the incident to the boy's mother.

"Your job is to keep my son out of harm's way," Tyne Clunch responded.

"I apologize for that, ma'am," Margaret acknowledged. "But I'm worried about Eugene's interaction with wildlife. I don't think he was in danger. I hate to say it, but I believe the boy *enjoyed* scaring that poor bird."

"The bird attacked *him*. He protected himself while his nanny was nowhere to be found," Tyne recapped. "He released the bird. It flew away uninjured. It made Eugene cry."

"Crocodile tears. I don't buy that he was truly upset," Margaret said.

"The boy suffered a trauma," Tyne insisted. "He was in shock. End of story."

Margaret recommended therapy for Eugene, but Tyne dismissed it as an overreaction.

"He's my son. I know him better than anyone."

"Of course, don't mean to overstep," Margaret conceded. "I suppose he did release the bird, eventually. No harm done."

The bird fiasco was a blip on an otherwise pleasant nanny experience for Margaret. She felt bad for the kid, who got dealt a pair of cruddy parents. She did, however, cease referring to Eugene as "Wily Gene" to wash away any reminders of the harrowing episode.

One of the women Tyne detested at the yacht club, Deirdre Fox, organized a lemonade sale for members' children. Kids were encouraged to mix batches of lemonade and set up stands alongside the clubhouse. The proceeds from the event would be donated to a charity, but Tyne was unsure of the specific cause.

"It's this Saturday, Eugene," Tyne told him. "Margaret will make lemonade for you and help you set up your stand."

"I don't want to do a lemonade stand," Eugene whined.

"You will," Tyne insisted. "I won't hear about Deirdre Fox's little snot-nosed brat's charitable efforts while my son is marked absent."

Whitford, home for the week, enforced Tyne's ruling and warned Eugene against upsetting his mother.

Margaret took Eugene to the fruit market and showed him how to pick out the juiciest lemons. Eugene and his nanny spent the morning before the event squeezing a tart batch of fresh lemonade. Margaret dropped him at the club and wished him luck. Eugene's lemonade won first place for overall taste. He ran to the clubhouse to show his parents the blue ribbon.

"How much money did you rake in?" Whitford asked.

"Thirty-one dollars," Eugene reported.

"How much did Rosalyn Fox raise?" Tyne inquired.

"Forty-five dollars," Eugene said. "Her's didn't taste as good, though. She used a mix."

Whitford set down his newspaper and looked Eugene in the eye.

"Your opponent's mix cost less, and she made a bigger profit," Whitford said.

"I won the prize," Eugene contended. "Blue ribbon."

"You spent twelve dollars on lemons and made thirty-one dollars. Your competition spent five dollars and made forty-five dollars," Whitford calculated. "There's a lesson there, son."

"I'll never hear the end of this from Deirdre," Tyne rolled her eyes. "Her little angel raising all that money for poor people and whatnot."

Margaret picked Eugene up from the club at the designated time and spotted the award in his box of supplies.

"Blue ribbon!" she exclaimed. "Winner, winner, chicken dinner!"

"I don't want chicken," Eugene whined.

"Geez, Grumpy Gus over here," Margaret said. "Who spit in your lemonade?"

Margaret was observant of the family dynamic, so it wasn't a big leap to assume Whitford and Tyne Clunch dismissed Eugene's victory.

"How about pizza?" she suggested. "Pizza for the blue ribbon winner."

Eugene wasn't allowed pizza, per his parents' rules. They considered it junk food unworthy of their station in society. Margaret figured a rebellious act might do wonders for the kid's self-esteem. She took Eugene to Next Door Pub and ordered the Moo-La Geneva, a five-cheese pizza specialty. Margaret requested everyone in the restaurant raise a glass to the lemonade champion,

Eugene. She purposely omitted the boy's surname, as the Clunch bloodline didn't elicit goodwill amongst locals. Patrons and servers congratulated Eugene on his accomplishment.

A week later, Eugene asked Margaret to take him back for more of the yummy contraband cuisine. They made Next Door Pub their regular haunt.

"Don't be telling your parents," Margaret winked. "They'll buy me a one-way train ticket back to Cohasset."

Eugene earned good grades at Gygax High School. Whitford wondered if his son might have a dash of the legendary Clunch acumen for wheeling and dealing. He enrolled Eugene in a Clunch-sponsored club for aspiring entrepreneurs, ages fifteen through eighteen. An unusually animated Eugene returned home from one particularly exciting club meeting, at which a contest for young marketers and innovators was announced. The youth who pitched the best business idea would win startup money and a meet-and-greet with Herb Kohl of Kohl's department store fame. The competition was months away, but Eugene couldn't wait to get started. All he needed was an idea for a business that could thrive in the fast-paced 1990s and into the approaching millennium. Margaret helped him brainstorm.

"Movie rentals mailed to your house?" Margaret thought out loud. "Eh. Scratch that. Folks like to wander around Blockbuster Video on a Friday night. I know I do. Gets me outta the house. The Blockbuster is so bright and clean."

"How about a new toy for kids?" Eugene asked.

"Make your own teddy bear?" Margaret suggested. "Fill it with stuffing and dress it in an outfit of your choosing. Could be neat o Although the toy store has teddy bears that are pre-stuffed and ready to cuddle. Yeah, forget it. That's no good."

"I'm never gonna come up with a great business!" Eugene screeched. "All my ideas stink!"

"Simmer down, Eugene," Margaret said. "Go take a walk around town. Find inspiration."

Eugene wandered down Main Street. Summering Illinois families shopped for sand shovels and boogie boards at the beach store. Men loaded cases of beer and bags of ice into car trunks. Couples strolled arm-in-arm. Eugene bought an orange Push-Up Pop from the ice cream cart and took a seat on a bench outside the animal hospital. A big-haired woman exited the veterinary clinic carrying a dachshund in her arms. She took a seat next to Eugene and positioned the dog on her lap.

"One pill per day, Rollie," the woman told the dachshund. "Doctor's orders."

She unscrewed the top of a medicine bottle and poured a fat, white pill into her palm. She shoved the pill into Rollie's mouth and clenched his jaw shut for several seconds. When she was satisfied, she released her hold. A slimy, saliva-covered pill dropped from Rollie's tongue onto the pavement below.

"Swallow it, Rollie!"

The woman tried again with the same result. Rollie rejected his medicine.

"Pardon me, lady," Eugene interrupted. "Have you tried hiding the pill in a glob of cheese?"

"Oh, yes," she said. "Rollie's nose is too good. He eats the cheese and spits out the pill. Same deal with peanut butter. He can sniff out the medicine."

Eugene looked down at his Push-Up Pop.

"What about orange sherbet?" he asked.

The woman decided it was worth a go. She handed the pill to Eugene, who buried it in the Push-Up Pop. The cold sherbet appealed to Rollie. Unfortunately, the dachshund found the hidden pill and spit it on the ground again.

"There's no fooling Rollie," the woman laughed. "He sure liked that sherbet, though. They oughta make a meat-flavored popsicle for dogs. That's a million-dollar idea right there. C'mon, Rollie, let's get you home."

Rollie stared at Eugene as he was carried away by the woman.

"Thanks, Rollie," Eugene whispered.

The Clunch household employed a chef named Hubert Ellis. Hubert arrived each day at five o'clock in the morning. At six o'clock, Hubert served bacon and eggs to Whitford Clunch (if Whitford happened to be in town). Margaret escorted Eugene downstairs at half past seven for cinnamon oatmeal. Tyne Clunch preferred French Toast and brunched after ten in the morning. Lunch and dinner followed a similar scattered schedule for the Clunch family. Following Tyne's late dinner, Hubert arranged snacks on the main staircase landing in case a Clunch family member got the late-night munchies. The kitchen went dark when Hubert ended his workday at eleven o'clock.

Hubert's last day in the employ of the Clunch household began like any other. He arrived on time and prepared bacon and eggs for Whitford Clunch, along with the iced coffee Whitford drank on humid summer mornings. Mid-breakfast, Whitford let out pained yelp loud enough to wake even Tyne from her fermented slumber. Tyne and Eugene Clunch descended the stairs and rushed into the kitchen. Hubert and all the other staff members, including Margaret, bowed their heads in front of an irate Whitford Clunch.

"Step forward and admit your guilt," Whitford demanded. "Or everyone's pay will be docked."

A cranky Tyne wanted to know what caused the commotion.

"Someone poisoned my coffee!" Whitford alleged.

Tyne perked up.

"What kind of poison?" she wondered.

"An unknown allergen," Whitford sneezed. "With a foul taste!"

Whitford paced back and forth, folding and unfolding his embroidered handkerchief.

"Who brought Mr. Clunch his coffee this morning?" Tyne interrogated.

"It was me, ma'am," Hubert raised his hand. "Same as usual."

"Hubert would never harm me," Whitford wiped at his eyes. "He's one of my closest friends,"

Hubert wasn't Whitford's friend; he was his employee. But Whitford was correct in his evaluation of Hubert's character. A conscientious chef like Hubert would never have willfully contaminated the coffee. The fact that Whitford Clunch was ungenerous of both spirit and salary didn't chisel away Hubert's ethics.

"Blast your benevolence," Tyne scolded her husband. "You're too tolerant and kind-hearted. Employees are bound to take advantage of your magnanimous nature."

Head still bowed, Margaret's eyes rolled. She was able to avoid audibly ridiculing Tyne's off-base character assessment of Whitford, a feat Margaret accomplished by biting her own tongue with such tenacity she nearly drew blood.

"You're right, dear," Whitford sniffled. "Got me pegged."

"Make him reenact the crime," Tyne instructed.

"That hardly seems necessary," Whitford said.

"They do it on *Murder, She Wrote*," Tyne circled the room. "Jessica Fletcher always gets her man."

"Very well," Whitford relented. "Show us the coffee routine, Hubert."

Hubert filled a ceramic cup with coffee from the pot. He went to grab ice but gasped when the freezer fog parted. Hubert picked up the ice tray. The frozen cubes were brown in color. Hubert showed Whitford.

"What the devil? Lord, what have I ingested?" Whitford cried.

"Appears to be beef broth, sir," Hubert assessed. "The kitchen was still dark when I iced your coffee. I didn't notice..."

"'Didn't notice,'" Tyne raised doubt. "That's your story, Hubert? How does one not notice brown ice?"

Hubert hung his head.

"I make no excuse, ma'am. Overtired, I suppose. Wasn't paying careful attention."

"Preparing safe meals is your one and only duty!" Tyne raged. "My husband could've been killed, leaving me a widow to raise our son on my own! All as a result of your incompetence. Shame on you, Hubert."

Tyne's exaggerations were normally a behind-her-back source of humor for the staff members. But none were tempted to giggle at this outrageous browbeating. Margaret couldn't hold her tongue any longer.

"No one is at death's door, ma'am," Margaret interjected. "Beef broth is heavy in histamines, which I'd categorize as inconvenient rather than deadly. Couple doses of Benadryl, and Mr. Clunch will be ship-shape."

"How dare you minimize this crime!" Tyne's barbaric temper flared. "Out of the kitchen, you! Bring Eugene outside for fresh air. I don't want him to suffer through this ordeal."

Margaret's instinct was to argue right versus wrong, but with her paycheck in peril, she thought better of it. She patted Hubert's shoulder in a show of support and led Eugene out to the front porch of the Clunch estate. Eugene swung on the porch swing.

Ten minutes later, Hubert emerged with a box of his belongings.

"Tell me you didn't fall on your spatula, Hubert. Reason with Mr. Clunch after the missus returns to her daily slumber," Margaret beseeched him.

"It's no use," Hubert said. "Better one of us is fired than all of us lose our jobs. In need of a fresh start, anyhow. I'll land on my feet."

"Beef juice in the ice tray," Margaret shook her head. "How in blazes does that happen?"

"Haven't the foggiest," Hubert half-chuckled.

Hubert hugged her goodbye and gave the seated boy a nod. Eugene's focus was on something behind Hubert, who turned around to follow the boy's gaze. The front gate was open, and a Crown Victoria with police markings sped up the winding driveway. The Crown Vic came to a stop near the porch steps, and two uniformed officers exited the vehicle. Tyne Clunch whipped open the front door and pointed at Hubert.

"Arrest him, officers! Attempted murder!"

"Let's remain calm," the older officer said. "What exactly happened?"

"He poisoned Whitford Clunch!" Tyne screeched. "A pillar of the community. Whitford Clunch, who hosts police fundraisers and contributed to the mayor's re-election campaign. Now, arrest this man, or you might as well hand over your badges,"

"This is ridiculous," Margaret intervened. "She's blowing this way outta proportion, officers. Mrs. Clunch is still loopy from last night's box of White Zinfandel."

Mrs. Clunch charged at Margaret and yanked the nanny's hair while screaming with rage. The policemen raced in to break up the assault. They instructed Mrs. Clunch to stand far apart from Margaret.

"Arrest her, too!" Mrs. Clunch shrieked. "The nanny! She conspired with the chef!"

"This lady has gone goobers," Margaret laughed. "Next she'll accuse the plastic lawn flamingos of being in the grassy knoll the day Kennedy was shot."

The younger police officer stifled a smile as his partner pulled him away to confer privately. The officers came to a consensus, and the older officer addressed the citizens on the porch.

"Hubert, why don't you come down to the station so we can discuss this matter in a safe environment? We can set you up with an attorney if you see fit."

"No need for a lawyer," Hubert said. "Nothing to hide."

"Ladies, please promise to keep your distance from one another," the older officer said. "Let's not complicate this situation."

Hubert ducked into the back of the police cruiser. Tyne cinched her robe and walked toward the front door. She remained silent, eyes on Margaret as she disappeared into the house. Margaret turned to Eugene, who continued swinging to and fro.

"Sorry you had to see all that nastiness," she said. "What a wacky way to start the day."

Eugene nodded. Margaret studied his reaction for signs of trauma from the frightening events of the morning, but she read his stoicism as something else entirely.

"Do you have any idea how beef broth ended up in the ice tray, Eugene?"

Eugene, still swinging on the bench, shook his head.

Margaret was suspended without pay for three days as a result of her insolence. On the fourth day, Margaret returned and noticed Hubert's blue Chevrolet Beretta still parked in the employee lot. A housekeeper heard Hubert had been formally charged for the beef broth incident.

"Attempted murder," the housekeeper whispered. "Of Whitford Clunch."

Margaret was tempted to march into Tyne Clunch's bedroom and smack some sense into the "bitter wino hagfish," but instead she focused her energy on helping Hubert. She called every criminal defense lawyer in the Yellow Pages until she found a reputable litigator who wasn't afraid of Whitford Clunch. Margaret met with the attorney, Alfred Mackerel, in person. Mackerel had thick eyebrows, calloused hands, and a scratchy voice marinated in life experience.

He welcomed Margaret into his second-floor office and listened as she detailed Hubert's case. The manner in which Mackerel digested the details and asked follow-up questions gave Margaret confidence she'd discovered a gem of a legal representative. Mackerel was incensed at the injustice. He spoke with substance. Mackerel displayed an innate understanding of the millstones of tolerance and subjugation thrust upon the backs of people who worked for a living, as opposed to people who needn't hoist a pebble to survive. Mackerel insisted on defending Hubert pro bono. Truth was, he was happy for the chance to face off with Whitford Clunch.

"Clunch stiffed my father's contracting business. Withheld payment after the job was done," Mackerel said. "Flat-out refused to pay based on some poppycock rationale. The man is a scoundrel. Personally, I wish someone had slipped him something stronger than beef broth. Rat poison would've been my choice. Although I fear Whitford Clunch has built up an immunity to the stuff, as the biggest rats tend to do."

The assistant district attorney wouldn't admit it, but she knew the case against Hubert was a sham. The judge knew it was a sham. The police officer who testified knew it was a sham. But the powers that be needed to placate Whitford Clunch. Whitford Clunch needed to placate Tyne Clunch. And Tyne Clunch needed to satisfy a dark desire to cause human suffering. Therefore, the charade commenced.

Alfred Mackerel's opening statement was fierce yet understated. He jabbed with the precision and power of legendary Chicago boxer Packey McFarland.

"Ladies and gentlemen of the jury, I regret the fact that the State has dragged you here today to waste your time on a case they know does not rise to the level of criminal activity. This was no more than a prank. A prank akin to unscrewing the cap on a salt shaker. Ever done that? Unscrew the top of a salt shaker? I tell you, I pulled that prank my father. He ended up with a mountain of salt on his pork chop. The look he gave me...boy oh boy. I never did that again."

The gallery erupted in laughter.

"Another time," Mackerel continued, "I put a rubber spider in my sister's dollhouse, and she beat me up. That's right. My sister beat me up. And guess what? I deserved it."

The jurors were in stitches. Mackerel had them eating out of his hand, awaiting the next punchline. Mackerel shifted to a solemn tone and confided in the jury.

"The victim of this particular prank was not Whitford Clunch. The only victim was Hubert Ellis, a loyal employee, a beloved co-worker, a diligent chef, a family man, and a man of impeccable ethics. Hubert Ellis, unaware of the tainted ice cubes, was set up by an unknown prankster. As a result of this prank, here's what happened: Whitford Clunch went golfing that very afternoon, with a minor case of the sniffles due to the unexpected histamines. Hubert Ellis, meanwhile, lost his job, had his name sullied with a ridiculous criminal charge, and had to ask his eighty-year-old mother to put her house up for bail money. Hubert Ellis, the only person to suffer any real-life consequences, now has his fate in your hands, ladies and gentlemen. The evidence against Hubert Ellis is circumstantial. There are zero witnesses of substance, and there is no conceivable reason to believe that Hubert Ellis had any knowledge of this alleged beverage tainting. Dozens of individuals had access to the Clunch freezer. Even Whitford Clunch refused to implicate his longtime chef and confidant. I know you'll use your best judgment and clear Hubert Ellis of all charges, because unlike my rubber spider and me, Hubert Ellis is innocent of wrongdoing."

The trial proceeded. Mackerel sliced and diced the prosecution's case into bologna like a skilled butcher at Usinger's Famous Sausage. Margaret testified for the defense. The jury needed less than an hour to declare Hubert "Not Guilty" of all charges. As Hubert's family embraced him, Tyne Clunch strutted defiantly down the aisle in her chinchilla wrap. Margaret, in celebration, mocked the defeated elitist with a subtle version of Madonna's "Vogue" pose. Tyne momentarily stopped in her tracks but resumed her departure after shooting Margaret an evil stare. Whitford Clunch, furtively pleased with the verdict but at the same time embarrassed about his involvement in the farce, couldn't muster the courage to look Alfred Mackerel in the eye, scurrying past the plucky attorney with his head down.

One week after Hubert was vindicated, Margaret's presence was requested in the dining room. She was surprised to see all three members of the Clunch family sitting down together for a meal prepared by the new house chef.

"Please join us, Margaret," Tyne Clunch smiled. "I figured it's about time we started eating together as a family. Before long, Eugene will be off to college."

Margaret took a seat next to Eugene and unfolded the cloth napkin for her lap.

"I owe you an apology, Margaret," Tyne said. "We haven't always seen eye-to-eye. And it's entirely my fault. Hostility is my cross to bear, according to my therapist. I've directed venom at you far too often."

"Not at all, ma'am," Margaret said. "But thank you."

"I'm turning over a new leaf," Tyne declared. "When I think of everything you've done for Eugene, I realize we owe you a debt of gratitude."

"Eugene's a heckuva kid. A pleasure," Margaret responded.

Tyne began weeping. Whitford picked up his Manhattan and studied the glass. Tyne's blubbering echoed off the walls. Margaret rose from her seat and offered Tyne a comforting pat on the back.

"The burden is so heavy lately," Tyne sobbed. "Thank you for understanding."

Tyne composed herself, and the attention turned to the extravagant meal. Margaret dug into the prime rib and scalloped potatoes. Tyne cut herself off after one glass of wine and even led a lively dinner discussion about the plight of the snow leopard, which she'd read about in a magazine. Margaret was mildly impressed. Before she excused herself for the evening, Tyne proclaimed that weekly dinners with Margaret were a new tradition for the Clunch family. So it was, every Thursday night Margaret dined with the Clunch bunch.

Margaret noted Tyne's sunnier disposition and sudden engagement with Eugene. She started to wonder if people could change. Margaret still harbored a fair amount of resentment on Hubert's behalf, but the grudge grew less prominent as the calendar turned pages. She started looking forward to the multi-course dinners and French wines.

One such evening, as Margaret scraped the bottom of her tiramisu dish, Eugene made an announcement. He had finalized his entry for the young innovators contest. This caught Whitford's ear. The family patriarch folded down the *Milwaukee Journal-Sentinel* and looked across the table.

"Care to pull back the curtain, Eugene?" Whitford refilled his pipe with tobacco. "Give us a preview of your big idea?"

"Pup Pops! Meat-flavored popsicles for dogs!" Eugene announced.

Whitford Clunch was underwhelmed. He lit the pipe and picked up his periodical. From behind the newspaper, the table heard Whitford's opinion.

"Americans will never spend hard-earned money on frivolous extravagances for pets."

Eugene's heart sank, but Tyne threw him a life preserver.

"I, for one, think it's an ingenious idea, Eugene!"

"Meat-flavored popsicles?" Margaret's face turned red. "Like the frozen beef broth that got pinned on Hubert?"

The table fell silent. Neither Hubert nor the beef cubes had been mentioned in the Clunch household since the trial ended.

"That's where I got the idea," Eugene claimed. "I thought dogs might like the taste."

Margaret was highly skeptical of Eugene's timeline, but Tyne's joy swept through the dining room like the wind off Lake Michigan.

"Marvelous, my dear," Tyne applauded. "Turning a negative into a positive. Isn't that splendid, Whitford?"

"Quite," Whitford peered over his paper. "Lemons into lemonade. Bravo, my boy."

"I have many friends at the club who indulge their doggies. I think you should reconsider your knee-jerk assessment, Whitford," Tyne urged.

"Of course," Whitford agreed. "Looking at it from another angle, you're definitely onto something there, Eugene. Keep at it, son. Kudos."

Eugene bounced in his chair with excitement, and Tyne proposed a toast to the young inventor in the family. Margaret chugged her chardonnay in one massive gulp.

The competition took place underneath the gazebo at Flat Iron Park. Participants decorated tables with glittery signs and printed banners. Parents and judges wandered from station to station as kids pitched and demonstrated. A youth draped in tie-dye wanted to open a Birkenstock-refurbishing storefront in Madison. A girl from Genoa City dreamed of funding a museum based on *The Young and the Restless*—a soap opera based in her hometown. A steadfast pair of siblings from Elkhorn fixated on research money for tracking werewolves.

Eugene's Pup Pops demonstration paled in comparison to the spectacle at TABLE #9, where Roslyn Fox set up shop. Roslyn's presentation got an assist from her older sister Gwen, an aspiring model working the advertising circuit in Chicago. (Deirdre Fox constantly bragged about Gwen's modeling to Tyne, who liked to burst Deirdre's bubble by inquiring why Gwen had only made it as far as Chicago as opposed to Paris or Milan.) Gwen and her model friends strutted up and down the pavilion, sporting Roslyn's business idea: mini-backpacks.

"It's like a backpack, only smaller," Roslyn announced. "It's more fashionable with its long straps."

"Can it hold your books?" a fellow student asked.

"If the books are small enough, then yes," Rosyln answered.

A George Michael song blared from the speakers as the models modeled. The fashion-forward jostled to be first in line to place an order with Roslyn. Tyne Clunch, who insisted on accompanying Eugene to the event, told him to pack up his display.

"Show's over," Tyne muttered. "Roslyn's the victor, again. Despite the fact her bags are cheap. They'll disintegrate after a month of wear."

Eugene boxed up his Pup Pops as the judge announced the winners.

"Our runner up is Eugene Clunch and his Puppy Pops!"

"Fix your hair before you go up there to accept second place," Tyne instructed.

Eugene lassoed his frizzy 'do with Margaret's homemade hair tie and approached the podium.

"Congratulations, Eugene Clunch," the judge said, handing him a ribbon.

"What's that in your hair?" Gwen Fox inquired.

Before Eugene could answer, the statuesque model advanced on him to get a close-up of the spongy accessory.

"The answer to my prayers!" Gwen exclaimed. "Does it yank on your scalp?"

Eugene shook his head. The gaggle of models gathered around Eugene, admiring the fashion statement.

"What do you call it?" Gwen asked.

"It's called a 'Clunchie'!" Tyne Clunch shouted from the back. "I invented it."

"Clunchie," Gwen repeated. "I need one!"

"I need a Clunchie too," another model echoed.

"Of course," Tyne smiled. "I'll take your orders over here."

The crowd abandoned the miniature backpack table and rushed over to Tyne, who basked in the attention. She crossed out `Pup Pops` atop Eugene's order form and scribbled in `Clunchie`. Even Deirdre Fox wanted one, an order Tyne was all too happy to fulfill.

Tyne convinced Whitford to contact a manufacturer that could begin pumping out Clunchies. Whitford also leased a storefront on Main Street and staffed it so Tyne wouldn't have to get her hands dirty. Word spread about the tiny marvel, and the Clunchie biz boomed.

Margaret remained unaware of the new branch of the Clunch empire until she strolled down Main Street on her lunch break one day. She noticed a flurry of commerce. Girls emerged from the Clunchie store sporting a hair tie that Margaret recognized as her own invention. That night, at the Clunch family dinner, she demanded answers.

"Did I hear you correctly, dear Margaret?" Tyne played coy. "You're laying claim to the Clunchie?"

"Darn tootin,'" Margaret said. "After all, I fashioned the darn thing."

"Not according to the patent office," Tyne smirked.

Margaret felt the room closing in on her.

"Eugene, tell your mom and dad the story," Margaret implored him.

"Go ahead, Eugene," Tyne grabbed her son's hand. "Tell the truth, now."

"I remember," Eugene began. "Mom combing my hair. She called me 'Wily Gene' because my hair was so unruly. She sewed together a stretchy fabric to tame my wily locks."

"Very good, honey," Tyne smiled. "Mommy is so proud of you. Daddy, too."

"That's my boy. The next great Clunch in a long line of Clunches," Whitford nodded.

"Now that's settled," Tyne unsheathed her utensils. "Shall we dine?"

Margaret felt dizzy.

"I've lost my appetite," she said.

"Speaking of appetites spoiled," Tyne replied. "I understand you've introduced our son to junk food, Margaret. Pizza at a local watering hole? You know greasy food is strictly forbidden."

Eugene refused to look at Margaret, who muttered "tattletale" under her breath. Tyne nibbled on an asparagus spear and pointed her fork at Margaret.

"Hate to be a stickler, but maintaining a consistent diet for Eugene is a priority. Rules are rules, and therefore you'll be terminated from our employ, Margaret. Please feel free to stay the night and leave first thing in the morning. On behalf of both Whitford and Eugene, I thank you for your years of service. As a token of our appreciation, we've gifted you with a Mackinac Island windbreaker. It's being packed in your suitcase as we speak, along with your other personal items."

Margaret didn't bother excusing herself from the table. She grabbed her suitcase and dragged it to the employee parking lot. On her way out of town, Margaret stopped at a Kwik Trip to fuel up and call her sister from the payphone.

"Debbie," Margaret sighed. "It's Peg."

There was no need to use her professional name "Margaret" when talking to her sister. Debbie sensed something was amiss.

"What's the matter, Peggy? Is everything alright?"

"I'm fine. Decided to move back to Minnesota. Can you help me find an apartment in The Cities?"

"Of course, Peggy. Anything you need."

With that, Margaret, aka Peggy, drove home to Minnesota for a fresh start. Her spirits were buoyed by the opportunity to reconnect with her sister and brother-in-law, not to mention her five nephews and her funny little niece, Anna.

Eugene matriculated to University of Iowa to study business. He was assigned his own room at Mayflower Residence Hall but shared a connected bathroom with two freshmen Film majors. One was a native of Alaska, and the other hailed from Hawaii.

"Do you like pizza, Eugene?" his Alaskan suitemate asked.

"I do," Eugene said. "Mind you, Malamute, I'm from the land of cheese."

"Lucky dog," his Hawaiian suitemate nodded. "You must've had so many places to choose from..."

"Actually, Clownfoot, I'd get the same thing every time from the same place: a five-cheese pizza from Next Door Pub."

Clownfoot was stunned.

"You've only tried one pizza your entire life? No toppings ever?"

"Am I missing out?" Eugene wanted to know.

"You're neglecting a world of possibilities! I'm speechless, Eugene!" Clownfoot exclaimed. "By the way, Eugene is a boring name. You need a nickname."

"A friend used to call me 'Wily Gene.'"

"I love it!" Clownfoot clapped. "From now on, you're known only as 'Wily Gene.'"

BRRRRRRRRRRRIIIIINNNGGGGG!!

The Malamute heard the loud dorm phone ringing in his room and hurried next door to answer the call. Wily Gene and Clownfoot heard an excited yelp. The Malamute received unexpected news: He'd been named the next Iowa City Pizza Steward.

"Left Said Fred failed out of school. I'm on deck! It's my turn!" The Malamute reported.

The Malamute was on cloud nine. He danced around, hugged Clownfoot, and then wrapped his gangly arms around Wily Gene.

People rarely hugged Wily Gene. He wasn't very huggable, truth be told. His parents never hugged him. In fact, the hug from The Malamute was only the third hug he'd been a part of over the course of his entire lifetime. The first hug was from nanny Margaret on her first day as a Clunch employee. Margaret was later reprimanded by Wily Gene's mother for the display of unwarranted affection. The second hug was a fluke, when an inebriated woman at his parents' yacht club mistook preteen Wily Gene for a famous jockey. The third hug was from The Malamute.

Is this friendship? Wily Gene wondered.

The Malamute's right-hand man, Clownfoot, was a readymade Chief Connoisseur. To fill out the team, they spent the next few weeks recruiting worthy pizza hounds who frequented local parlors. With the last remaining spot on the Connoisseur roster, The Malamute wanted to take a chance on Wily Gene. He discussed the possibility with Clownfoot in private.

"I have my doubts. Wily is a pizza hack. A budlacker," Clownfoot debated.

"But a quick study," The Malamute countered. "Under your tutelage, Clownfoot, even Wily can become a worthy Connoisseur."

"Aw, shucks," Clownfoot blushed. "You sold me, buddy. I'll take the amateur under my wing."

They approached Wily Gene, who accepted the invite to join The Malamute's probationary Connoisseur squad. The Malamute placed his hands on Wily Gene's shoulders

"Stick with us, Wily Gene. You'll be a regular aficionado by the time we're done with you."

"I'm in your hands, my friends," Wily Gene said.

As promised, The Malamute and Clownfoot educated Wily Gene. The novice learned about New Haven apizza and Jersey Shore boardwalk slices. They taught him the differences between stuffed, deep dish, and pan pizza. Wily Gene found lessons on toppings and combos especially enlightening.

"Observe how the onions bring out the best in the sausage," The Malamute noted.

"Same principle applies to green peppers and pepperoni," Clownfoot added.

"Interesting," Wily Gene said. "Theoretically, the flavor combinations are endless."

"Conceivably, sure," Clownfoot allowed. "But don't go overboard."

"I want another slice of yesterday's deep dish," Wily Gene licked his lips.

Wily Gene opened the refrigerator in his kitchenette, but the pizza was gone.

"I finished off your leftovers," Clownfoot said. "My bad."

"Not to worry, friend," Wily Gene smiled.

They introduced Wily Gene to the other pre-Connoisseurs, including Cloris, Jenga Jim, and Cheez Louise. Cheez Louise gave Wily Gene a welcome-to-the-club hug, his fourth all-time. Wily Gene was starting to rack up the hugs.

Retiring Steward Left Said Fred passed out study materials so the prospective Connoisseurs could learn the history of Secret Pizza. Wily Gene stayed up all night reading. He heard Clownfoot stirring in the bathroom the next morning and flung open the door. Clownfoot was gargling.

"Good morning, Clownfoot!"

Clownfoot spit and wiped his mouth.

"You're in a good mood, Wily," he said.

"You should be, too. We're all gonna be filthy rich!" Wily Gene announced.

The Malamute overheard the conversation and entered the shared bathroom.

"Once we learn the secret behind Secret Pizza, we can sell it for big bucks," Wily Gene schemed.

Wily Gene tried to hug The Malamute, who pushed him away.

"That's not why we're doing this, Wily. You've got the wrong idea. Besides, isn't your family already wealthy?"

"Yes, but I want to create my own legacy."

"This ain't the way to get started. You're barking up the wrong tree, Wily," Clownfoot said.

Wily Gene slammed the door in Clownfoot's face.

An emergency meeting was called during which Wily Gene was expelled from the Connoisseurs. When The Malamute and Clownfoot returned to the dorm that night, Wily Gene's door was ajar, and all of his stuff was gone. He had quit school and returned home to Wisconsin.

Whitford Clunch was none too pleased with his dropout son. Whitford gifted the boy with a sailboat, in the hopes it might ignite a passion within his dullard of an heir. Wily Gene took sailing lessons as a youth, as all Clunch men did, but lacked an affinity for the sport. Nevertheless, Whitford Clunch insisted on a sailing trip in the south seas, just the two of them. Tragedy struck when Whitford succumbed to a bout of pneumonia somewhere in the Pacific Ocean. Despite the trauma of watching his father die, coupled with making the difficult decision to dump Whitford's body unceremoniously at sea, Wily Gene was able to conjure up his nautical know-how and guide the vessel to New Zealand. Wily Gene flew home to the United States to comfort his mother, who'd been battling a wicked cough. Wily Gene sat by her bedside, day and night. Less than a month after the death of her husband Whitford, Tyne Clunch stopped breathing in her sleep. Obligated yacht club members showed up at Tyne's service to pay respect.

"She's in a better place," Deirdre Fox managed.

Nineteen-year-old orphan Wily Gene was left in control of the Clunch family business holdings. He sold the Clunchie store and all its rights to the highest bidder. He put an immediate halt to all sailboat sponsorships, which caused quite the uproar amongst his late father's advisers. They begged him to reconsider, to no avail. Wily Gene was out to create his own legacy.

Wily Gene purchased a deserted diner and hired a team of contractors to refurbish the joint. Wily Gene's Pizza Canteen opened for business a year after his mother's funeral. He leased every available billboard in a thirty-mile area to promote the new pizzeria. The ads boasted topping combinations beyond the scope of any sane mind. On that promise, Wily Gene delivered. Unfortunately, his twisted pizza combos dissuaded repeat business and impeded word-of-mouth recommendations. He sank money from the family fortune into radio advertising, still convinced he'd entice enough exotic pizza fans to springboard the parlor's success. The freaky-tongued market that Wily Gene targeted never materialized.

Wily Gene's Pizza Canteen was a money pit and a failure. Wily Gene resigned himself to regrouping and reopening as either a coffee shop or a juice bar. That same day, two high school kids plopped down in a booth and requested a plain cheese pizza. Wily Gene ignored the order and hid in the back until they left his restaurant. The following day, the kids returned. The talkative one made outlandish claims about his quiet friend's abilities. Wily Gene was desperate enough to give the wallflower a chance. Theo, the new hire, required no learning curve. Wily Gene handed him the keys to the business, and the whiz kid proved to be a miracle worker. Instead of extreme ingredients, Theo insisted on simple, natural toppings. Wily Gene was reminded of his first pizza experience with Margaret.

"That's the ticket," Wily Gene declared. "The beauty is in the simplicity!"

"Don't discount quality," Theo cautioned. "Never skimp on quality ingredients."

Wily Gene advertised the menu changes, and hungry Sconnies flocked to the Canteen. Word got around, and Wily Gene's became a hot spot, with hour-long waits to be seated. Wily Gene was so appreciative of Theo's efforts that he bought him an expensive pair of NBA tickets to see his favorite team. He also gave Theo a large Christmas bonus, complete with a promise to hire him full-time as soon as he finished high school. Theo loved the work and admired the boss who believed in him.

That February, Theo noticed a change in the ingredients. The tomatoes seemed less plump. The olives didn't have the same luster. The onions were discolored. He knocked on Wily Gene's office door.

"Theo, my secret weapon! Come on in."

Theo noticed a manila envelope marked KMAP on Wily Gene's desk.

"What's 'KMAP'?" Theo asked.

Wily Gene shoved the envelope into a drawer.

"My guide map," Wily Gene explained. "I was waiting to surprise you with this news, but we're expanding. I purchased nine new storefronts across Wisconsin. And that's only the beginning!"

Theo was hesitant.

"Gradual expansion, one location at a time, would be prudent. Not so sure about nine new pizzerias all at once. Who's going to run them?"

"I'll hire cheap labor," Wily Gene said. "And we'll drop in for quality checks, of course."

"Speaking of quality, did we switch vegetable suppliers?" Theo asked. "I've noticed subpar veggies across the board."

Wily Gene assured Theo it was a temporary cost-cutting measure until the new locations were up and running. The boss promised that he would eventually reconnect with the vegetable farms Theo had sourced.

"Quality ingredients are the standard we built Wily Gene's reputation on," Theo argued. "Our regulars are going to notice."

"We're established," Wily Gene countered. "Grandfathered in as a quality place, with the advertising to drill it into the heads of the public. Plus, I lowered prices to the point of ridiculousness. We could replace our sausage with dog food and hear nary a complaint."

"Please tell me you're not using dog food," Theo said.

"Our meat supplier hasn't changed," Wily Gene smiled. "Nor will it. You have my word."

A month later, Wily Gene switched meat suppliers. The discounted pepperoni and sausage increased his bottom line. Theo could taste the difference, but customers kept ordering the affordable pizza. Wily Gene was right about the effective advertising. After the first nine franchises opened successfully, Wily Gene announced nine more. The rapid growth was astounding, considering the shape the business had been in less than a year prior. Clunch family money played a big role in the expansion. Plus, each store he opened earned Wily Gene more and more money to spend on advertising. Wily Gene adopted an outgoing persona and insisted on being the star of his own TV commercials. He designed orange denim jeans with tiny embroidered pizzas dotting the legs and buttocks.

He created a spray-painted "Wily Gene" T-shirt and wore silly goggles shaded to look like pizzas. He puffed up his frizzy hair into a massive round mound that rivaled PBS painter Bob Ross. In each ad, Wily Gene stepped out from behind a counter, revealing his unconventional pants.

"I'm Wily Gene, and these are my wild jeans!" he'd Bozo-cackle into the camera.

The pitchman would reach into his pocket and produce a cartoonishly large coupon.

"'Three Large Pepperoni Pizzas for $12'! Told you these jeans were wild! Don't miss out on this bonkers deal! Call Wily Gene's Pizza Canteen now!"

Sales skyrocketed. Wily Gene's ego blasted off too.

Theo hounded Wily Gene for answers about the ingredient supply. Wily Gene ran low on excuses. Theo finally cornered his boss one morning before the store opened. Theo was exasperated.

"Slimy mushrooms, frozen sausage—I can't take it any longer! I've set up meetings with our original suppliers. It's time to bring the quality back to Wily Gene's Pizza Canteen. Either that, or I quit."

Wily Gene wrote Theo a check for $100,000.

"What's this?"

"You've done so much for me, Theo," Wily Gene said. "But our goals no longer align. I accept your resignation."

With Theo out of his hair and his empire expanding, Wily Gene was ready for the next phase of his revenge plot against the Connoisseurs. Operation KMAP (Kill Mom And Pop) was proceeding even faster than he envisioned.

23

RACE TO CEDAR RAPIDS

February 8, 1997, Seven O'Clock At Night. Five Hours Until National Pizza Day

The Malamute and Clownfoot told Anna everything they knew or had heard about Wily Gene. The nugget about the Clunchie allowed Anna to finally piece together the full truth about her aunt's unethical former employer.

"I can't believe Wily Gene's family stole my Aunt Peggy's invention! Always wondered why she insisted I wear my hair down. She didn't want to be reminded of the Clunchie."

Clownfoot tried to make Anna feel better by offering her a sip of his Kiwi Strawberry Snapple.

"I don't want a Snapple," Anna refused. "I want to ram a Clunchie down Wily Gene's throat. Tell me where I can find him."

"No need to seek him out," Clownfoot said. "Wily Gene is coming for us. Hence the satellite surveillance. I fear J.R. and Crust are leading him to The Source as we speak. It could spell doom for Secret Pizza and the Connoisseurs. He'll stop at nothing to destroy us."

"Destroy us? Uff-da! You didn't think to mention any of this earlier?" Anna chastised. "*Hey, by the way, an unpredictable kook with unlimited resources might chase you down...*"

"In retrospect, it's a subject we should've broached," The Malamute admitted.

"It never came up naturally in conversation," Clownfood said.

"You oafs only cared about passing the baton," Anna clenched her teeth. "More than the safety of your replacements!"

The Malamute and Clownfoot bowed their heads in shame.

"You're right, Astronomer Anna," The Malamute whimpered. "We were selfish."

"Blinded by the quest and unconcerned with the consequences," Clownfoot concurred.

"What are the odds that Wily Gene wronged my aunt *and* Evan's best friend?" Anna thought out loud. "And then fate brought us together at Pagliai's in Iowa City."

Clownfoot made a pained sound, like he was dying of guilt. The Malamute elbowed him into silence. This interaction didn't go unnoticed by Anna. She lifted Clownfoot's chin and stared him down. Anna's direct eye contact was too much for Clownfoot to bear.

"I greased up Crust's Mountain Dew the day you met Evan. The pop slipped out of Crust's hands. You stepped in to help mop up the mess, and the rest is history."

"To what end?" Anna asked.

"Wily Gene's empire has infiltrated the state of Iowa, and Iowa City is next on his hit list," The Malamute explained. "In you and Evan, we saw two great pizza minds, both with an axe to grind against our mortal enemy. Of course we wanted you to be friends. The falling in love part, well, that was a happy byproduct of our meddling."

"You might even think of us as matchmakers," Clownfoot said. "Pizza cupids."

Clownfoot peeked at Anna, hoping for forgiveness. She shook her head at the hapless duo.

"C'mon, grab your coats," Anna instructed.

"Where are we going?" The Malamute asked.

"Astronomer Anna is gonna shove snow down our shirts," Clownfoot shivered. "And, frankly, we deserve it."

"You dodo birds are directing me to The Source," Anna said. "Although, I hate to abandon my post. It's important that someone record this data."

Professor Carson overheard Anna's dilemma. He offered to cover for her and record the data in her absence. Anna's inherent Midwest politeness wouldn't allow a favor to be bestowed without modest pushback.

"I can't ask you to do that, Professor," she said. "You're too kind. Besides, I'm sure your wife has a hot dish waiting for you at home."

"My wife gladly shares her astronomer husband with the night sky. In fact, at our wedding, the priest said, 'You may Coperni-kiss the bride.'"

Professor Carson paused for laughter, but Clownfoot and The Malamute stared blankly.

"Coperni-kiss," Professor Carson repeated. "Get it? Kiss the bride. Copernicus, the father of heliocentrism? Astronomy humor."

Clownfoot shrugged.

"I get it, Professor," Anna chuckled politely. "Very cute."

"We know the man who launched that satellite, Professor," The Malamute said.

"His name is Eugene Clunch," Clownfoot elaborated. "Also known as Wily Gene. He joined your Astronomy Club a few years back."

"Eugene Clunch," Professor Carson recalled. "That name rings a bell. Bright and ambitious student, but capricious. Commandeered the telescope with minimal regard for fellow stargazers."

"We're on a mission to confront him," Anna said. "Find out what his dealio is."

"Go on, Anna," Professor Carson insisted. "Find out the dealio and save the day. The stars will be waiting whenever you shall return."

Anna tossed her car keys to The Malamute.

"My green Jeep Cherokee is parked on Jefferson. Go warm it up, goofballs."

Anna placed a call to Trivia Trixie at the library and convinced her to ditch the remainder of her work shift. With the two pizza gurus in the back of her

Jeep, Anna scooped up Trixie at the library and headed northbound on I-380. Clownfoot briefed Trixie on the Wily Gene situation, then switched conversational gears.

"Heard you cut down Tommy Anchors in the trivia contest. No small feat."

"You heard right, Clownfoot," Trixie said. "Dropped Anchors."

"You're a trivia genius," Clownfoot declared.

"I don't know about that," Trixie blushed. "But here's a fun piece of trivia about Anna. Did you know her celebrity crush is Andre Agassi?"

Anna was proud to admit it.

"I'm not embarrassed. Andre Agassi is hot! Those Canon Rebel commercials when he was shirtless and sweaty. His super hairy chest..."

Anna and Trixie giggled at Anna's descriptive fantasy. Anna never had a problem laughing at herself.

"It occurs to me I don't know Trivia Trixie's preferred topping," Clownfoot realized. "I'm aware Astronomer Anna is all about the onions."

"Darn tootin,'" Anna confirmed.

"Pepperoni never fails," Trixie answered.

"Hear! Hear!" The Malamute trumpeted. "Pepperoni, America's most popular topping."

"Care to guess my favorite topping, Trivia Trixie?" Clownfoot asked.

"Don't say pineapple," The Malamute warned. "Clownfoot will lose his composure."

Clownfoot gave The Malamute a dirty look.

"I was gonna guess ham," Trixie said.

"That's correct!" Clownfoot exclaimed.

"I know," Trixie said. "Anna tipped me off."

"Ah," Clownfoot slumped back in his seat. "Well-played."

The Malamute snickered at the exchange. Clownfoot stared ahead out the front windshield and noticed a car with one burnt-out headlight.

"Badiddle!" he shouted, tapping the ceiling of the car with his fist.

Badiddle was a popular car game for night travelers. The game was initiated when an approaching car with only one functioning headlight was spotted.

The last rider to say "badiddle" and tap the ceiling was the loser. Keenly aware of the rules of the game, Anna and Trixie followed Clownfoot's lead, uttering "badiddle" and tapping the car ceiling.

"No fair," The Malamute groaned. "I wasn't paying attention."

"Don't be a sore loser," Clownfoot said. "Ready to accept your punishment?"

The Malamute steeled himself and presented his arm. Clownfoot punched him in the bicep.

"Ow! Go easy, Clownfoot," The Malamute winced. "I hate this game! Who cares if a car only has one headlight?"

Anna caught a glimpse of the vehicle as it crossed paths with her Jeep.

"That's a coinky-dink," Anna said. "You know the car with one headlight, the one we badiddled? It was a delivery guy for Wily Gene's Pizza Canteen."

"More than a coincidence. Wily could be tracking our movements," Clownfoot warned.

"Now, now. Let's not jump to conclusions," The Malamute urged. "There are Wily Gene's Pizza Canteen franchise locations in the area. That vehicle is likely out on a normal delivery. No biggie."

Clownfoot turned around to watch the Wily Gene's Pizza Canteen delivery vehicle out the back window. To calm Clownfoot's nerves, Trivia Trixie tossed him a brainteaser.

"This *Scream* actor's given name is Bryan Ray Trout. Do you know his screen name?"

Clownfoot kept his eyes fixated on the taillights of the delivery vehicle as he fielded the trivia question.

"Skeet Ulrich," he answered.

"Clownfoot is correct," Trixie confirmed. "Well done."

"Skeet Ulrich is also hot," Anna remarked. "I mean, he's no Agassi, but handsome."

Trixie and Anna chuckled as the Jeep continued its journey to Cedar Rapids.

24

GHOSTS OF BLANDVILLE

B landville was littered with abandoned storefronts and malfunctioning streetlights. We met Evan in front of B.J.'s Pizza, a by-the-slice joint with an "Out of Business" sticker strewn across its paint-chipped sign.

"Nothing sadder than a local pizzeria going out of business," I sighed.

"B.J.'s isn't the only casualty," Evan said.

He led us half a block down to Pizzeria Garza, another shuttered parlor. There was a "For Lease" sign next to calligraphy boasting:

`Blandville's Hometown Pizza!`

The Grappler Twins, Gil, and Hank wandered around the corner to explore more of Blandville's ruins while Evan and I pressed our noses up against the front window of Pizzeria Garza. I spotted framed photographs of Little League teams once sponsored by the establishment.

"The Malamute told me Blandville was infiltrated," Evan said.

"By whom?" I asked.

"Beats me," Evan shrugged.

Evan requested a moment of silence for Pizzeria Garza and B.J.'s Pizza. We bowed our heads until the silence was broken by Prankster Hank, who beckoned from the intersection of Chris Street and Gustafson Road.

"Guys, come check this out!"

Evan and I hustled down the dark Blandville block and turned onto Gustafson Road. A barrage of snowballs bombarded us when we rounded the corner. Prankster Hank giggled with his co-conspirators Chill Gil and the Grappler Twins. I brushed snow off my coat.

"Why do we always believe Prankster Hank?" Evan asked.

"He's very convincing," I said.

Prankster Hank handed Evan a bottle of Michael Jordan cologne.

"A gift for both of you," Prankster Hank said. "For being rock stars who know how to take a joke."

Evan spritzed himself and gave my partial beard a spritz too.

"Smells like greatness," Evan smiled. "Thanks, Prankster Hank."

"You're totally welcome, dudes," Prankster Hank said. "But there really is something around the next corner that you oughta see."

He gestured to the intersection of Gustafson Road and Clark Avenue.

"Do you think we were born yesterday?" Evan doubted.

"We're not falling for the same trick twice in a row," I said.

Prankster Hank gave us a charming smile.

"Guys, trust me."

Prankster Hank wasn't kidding this time. We turned onto Clark Avenue, where neon lights nearly blinded us. The glow emanated from the marquee of a Wily Gene's Pizza Canteen storefront. Evan was dumbfounded. He had no idea Wily Gene's empire had expanded beyond Wisconsin. A sign in the front window offered a ridiculous deal:

ANY LARGE PIZZA $3

"Three bucks? Almost *have* to get one for that price," Prankster Hank decided.

Chill Gil and Mike Grappler followed Hank inside the gaudy restaurant. The trio emerged ten minutes later with a box of Wily Gene's pizza. They each sampled a slice. Mike and Gil's expressions turned sour. Hank started dry heaving.

"This is bad," Chill Gil gagged. "Not a quality pizza."

"Worse than the pizza puff I found in J.R.'s glove compartment," Mike added.

"I keep those in there for emergencies," J.R. responded.

I collected the pizza box and tossed it in a dumpster. We walked back to Chris Street. Evan's car wouldn't start, so he made a quick payphone call, then squeezed in the back of J.R. Grappler's truck.

"Next stop, Cedar Rapids," J.R. announced.

25

UNSCRUPULOUS PUPIL

Professor Carson paged through the rolodex in his office until he found the card for the American Astronomical Society. He dialed the number but only reached an answering machine.

"Hi, this is Professor Carson at Van Allen Observatory in Iowa City, reporting an unauthorized satellite. One of my former students is conducting an illegal surveillance operation. I will send the coordinates via electronic mail. Thank you."

Professor Carson hung up the phone and turned his attention to leftover carne asada and rice. A shadow crept over his plate, and he heard a familiar voice in his ear.

"Tattling on your former student? I thought the skies belonged to all of us, Professor."

Professor Carson's fork dropped to the desk. He swiveled his chair to face Wily Gene, who wore his television pitchman costume complete with signature wild jeans and painted goggles. Wily Gene's hair formed a round, fluffy mound of frizz atop his head, like a dandelion right before the seeds drift away.

"Eugene Clunch! How did you get in here?"

"The door was open," Wily Gene said.

Professor Carson remembered he'd propped open the observatory door when Mrs. Carson dropped off his dinner.

"I see," Professor Carson said. "What can I do for you, Eugene?"

"For starters, you can stop tracking my satellite."

"I'm following protocol. All unsanctioned satellites must be reported."

Wily Gene moved his goggles to the top of his head and read Professor Carson's rolodex card.

"American Astronomy Association?" he laughed. "They can't stop me."

"The wheels are already in motion, Eugene," Professor Carson stated. "I'll see to it myself that your satellite doesn't violate anyone's privacy."

Wily Gene sneered.

"Then you leave me little choice, Iowa Jones," Wily Gene said.

"Did you call me 'Iowa Jones'? I don't get it."

Wily Gene redonned his goggles before he explained.

"Indiana Jones was a professor. You're a professor. Only we're in Iowa, not Indiana."

"That's a bit of a stretch," Professor Carson cringed. "Even for me, a proud purveyor of jokes that don't always land."

"It's a brainy witticism!" Wily Gene yelled. "Iowa Jones!"

"If you say so," Professor Carson shrugged.

"I'd like to hear you come up with something better," Wily Gene scoffed.

Professor Carson adjusted his sport coat as he accepted the challenge.

"Putting me on the spot here. How about Professor Tele-Dope? Mocks my intelligence while simultaneously deriding my chosen profession. Again, that's off the top of my head..."

"Enough banter, Professor. You're coming with us."

"Us?"

Two brawny brutes in decorative pizza jumpsuits barged into Professor Carson's office.

"Meet Pepperoni and Sausage," Wily Gene introduced his lackeys.

Pepperoni and Sausage forced the Professor out of his chair.

"You're kidnapping me?" he asked.

"Let's classify it as a field trip, Professor," Wily Gene cackled.

Pepperoni held Professor Carson's arms behind his back as Sausage threw his carne asada in the trash.

"Hey, that was my dinner!" Professor Carson protested.

"Don't worry. We'll grab a bite in Cedar Rapids," Wily Gene said.

They escorted Professor Carson out to a Wily Gene's Pizza Canteen van.

26

BRIDGE AND A BARN

J.R. Grappler's SUV cruised down a dark road on the outskirts of Cedar Rapids and slowed to a stop at a snowy bridge.

"This looks exactly like the bridge in the painting Trixie showed us," I said.

Mike Grappler exited the vehicle and jogged up to a snow-covered sign. He wiped the powder off and confirmed it was the Chiron Bridge. Mike jumped back in the SUV, and we drove across the bumpy but solid overpass. I made a mental note to tell LaTonya about the Chiron Bridge next time I called home.

Down the road a mile or so, Prankster Hank spotted a mural for Patterson Seeds featuring a smiling seed salesman.

"Stop the car!" Hank shouted. "Remind me, what was Chill Gil's clue?"

"Phat with a *P-H*." Gil said.

Prankster Hank pointed at the seed salesman on the welcome mural. The salesman wore a hat with the letter *P* for Patterson Seeds.

"Could it be *P*-hat?"

"*P*-dash-hat!" J.R. Grappler affirmed. "Nice catch, Prankster Hank."

"I have my moments," Hank tipped his cap.

J.R. turned left and parked in the unplowed lot of Patterson Seeds. The property appeared deserted. I hopped out the back passenger side and held the door open for Evan.

"Hey," I tapped Evan's arm. "Isn't that Anna's Jeep?"

Evan raced over to the Cherokee to confirm that it belonged to his girlfriend.

"Anna!" he screeched. "Where are you?"

"Over here, Evan!"

Anna waved from the lit doorway of a barn on the Patterson Seeds property. Evan dashed over and embraced her. The fellas and I jogged along behind him. Evan apologized to his girlfriend for abandoning her and leaving his friends to solve the Secret Pizza puzzles without his help.

"I'm sorry for bailing and acting flighty. Fortunately, I came to my senses and made a U-turn. I shouldn't have left without consulting you first, Anna Bear."

Anna forgave Evan and nuzzled him.

"You smell nice," Anna cooed.

"We got new cologne," I explained from over Evan's shoulder.

"How did you beat everyone here, Hot Lips?" Evan asked.

Anna walked us around the corner to a seating area where Trivia Trixie was refereeing an argument between The Malamute and Clownfoot.

"Glad you're all here to witness my roommate's absurdity," Clownfoot welcomed us. "My misguided friend, The Malamute, claims Kevin Nealon was a better *Weekend Update* host than *Saturday Night Live* legend Dennis Miller. Do go on, Malamute."

"Even Nealon's sign-off was better," The Malamute said.

"Better than Dennis Miller's iconic pen circle and toss?" Clownfoot disputed.

Clownfoot pretended to faint into my arms to illustrate his shock at The Malamute's contention.

"How do we all feel about the new host, Norm McDonald?" Trivia Trixie asked.

"I like Norm," The Malamute said.

Clownfoot awoke from his dramatic slumber and expressed enthusiasm for Norm too.

"Good. You agree on something," Trixie said. "Now let's complete this Secret Pizza mission so we can get back to our warm cars."

Prodded by Anna, The Malamute and Clownfoot repeated the story of Wily Gene's upbringing. The goofy gurus also confessed to withholding information and plotting to introduce Evan to Anna. Lovestruck Evan was awed by the serendipitous Wily Gene common ground he shared with Anna and therefore unbothered by The Malamute and Clownfoot's tactics.

"Wily Gene's Pizza Canteen. Sampled some of that so-called pizza in Blandville," Chill Gil reported. "Yuck."

"If you wandered down Chris Street in Blandville, you've seen the damage Wily Gene can do to a town," Clownfoot said. "He won't stop until he's run every local pizzeria out of business. We have reason to believe he's on his way here in an attempt to usurp the power of Secret Pizza and use it against us."

I couldn't bear the thought of Iowa City ending up like Blandville. I figured Wily Gene wouldn't stop there.

What's to prevent him from opening a shiny new storefront right next to Contadino's, knocking the tiny pizzeria out of business, and endangering LaTonya's livelihood?

27

GURUS ON GUARD

The only route to the Patterson Seeds property was by way of the Chiron Bridge. Clownfoot hustled toward the bridge to keep a lookout for Wily Gene. The Malamute lurked in the shadows beneath the Patterson Seeds mural, closer to The Source. This layered positioning was The Malamute's brainchild. He wanted to give our gang of aspiring Connoisseurs time to complete the final set of challenges. Wily Gene's old suitemates figured they could hold him off long enough to prevent him from accessing The Source while the portal opened briefly for Evan. The portal was only accessible once a year, just after midnight on National Pizza Day.

Clownfoot and The Malamute communicated via walkie-talkie.

"Come in Clownfoot, do you copy?"

"Copy, Malamute. I'm nearing the bridge."

"You're already at the bridge? That was quick, buddy."

"I'm fast. You'll recall I once beat All-American Tim Dwight in a footrace," Clownfoot bragged.

"You beat Tim Dwight because it was downhill in January, and your feet are like skis."

"Whatever. A win is a win."

Clownfoot stepped onto the edge of the Chiron Bridge and squinted across into the darkness. He saw no sign of Wily Gene or any approaching vehicles. In the very center of the bridge, however, he noticed an object sticking out of the snow. Clownfoot plodded through heavy powder to investigate. He kicked at the item, then wiped the top with his glove. It was a shoebox—a Reebok shoebox. Clownfoot's excitement mounted. The box contained a pair of Reebok Pumps, size 23. These weren't run-of-the-mill Reeboks one could buy at Nordstrom. They were limited edition Pumps inspired by Clownfoot's favorite film, *Above the Rim*. The shoe design was approved by Tupac Shakur himself. Giddiness overcame Clownfoot. He radioed The Malamute to inform him of the lucky discovery. The Malamute sensed danger.

"Run, Clownfoot! It's a trap!"

Clownfoot was too elated to be wary.

"Finders keepers, I say!"

The next sound The Malamute heard over the two-way radio was jumbled static. A panicked scream followed. The Malamute dropped his walkie-talkie in the snow and sprinted towards the Chiron Bridge.

"Hold on, Clownfoot! I'm coming!"

28

CORNY EQUINE SIDEKICK

February 8, 1997, Nine O'Clock At Night. Three Hours Until National Pizza Day

Trivia Trixie insisted we visit the stall of the lone horse in the barn. The equine's name was Pokey—same as the corny horse sidekick on the TV show *Gumby*.

"This handsome stallion is my clue," Trixie said. "Hiya, Pokey."

A goat meandered out from behind Pokey and licked my hand. I offered it a nearly empty can of Gloam Pop.

"Don't give her that, Crust," J.R. Grappler admonished. "Goats don't really eat aluminum. That's only in cartoons."

I apologized to the goat.

"I have a thought," Anna said. "Trixie's clue said we're supposed to find an equine sidekick. What if we interpret it as 'corny sidekick *to* the equine'? Therefore, the *goat* is the sidekick."

I checked the goat's name tag. Her name was Hokey, a synonym for corny.

"So..." Prankster Hank processed the new information. "We're supposed to do the Hokey Pokey?"

"Does anyone recall how the song goes?" Anna asked.

Mike Grappler remembered the sequencing and offered to lead the dance.

We circled up and started doing the Hokey Pokey. Our motions were methodical at the outset. Then Prankster Hank amped up his volume. Anna followed suit, and her robust singing voice made me chuckle. She inspired all of us to harmonize with added gusto. By the end of the dance, the entire squad was belting out the lyrics and shaking our butts with glee.

The song ended, and we froze. Smiles dwindled.

"Is something supposed to happen now?" J.R. Grappler asked.

A bright light suddenly shone from across the snowy field and moved towards us at a steady pace. A burly, middle-aged man in overalls carrying a flashlight entered the barn with a cheerful smile.

"Hi, guys! I'm Dusty!"

"We summoned Dusty when we did the Hokey Pokey," Prankster Hank supposed.

Dusty doubled over with laughter.

"I saw you all dancing! Funniest darn thing I've seen in all my years working here! Totally unnecessary. All you had to do was find the goat."

Dusty mimicked our Hokey Pokey dance and laughed himself silly.

"I'm not sure I like Dusty," Trivia Trixie opined.

"I'm sorry," Dusty gathered himself. "All in good fun. I'm only teasing."

"Dusty, are you...are you The Source?" Evan asked.

Dusty's expression grew serious. Evan held his breath in anticipation. Dusty couldn't keep a straight face, and he broke into another chuckle.

"Heck no! Just an Iowa guy who loves pizza. I've been the caretaker here for decades. You are getting closer to The Source, however."

Dusty pointed his puffy forefinger out the back door of the barn. Beyond a snowy patch of tundra, there was a mystifyingly lush cornfield.

"Corn grows in the winter here, apparently," J.R. Grappler noted.

'It's a magical place," Dusty smiled.

"How did Wily Gene's satellite not single out a thriving cornfield amongst the snow?" Anna wondered.

"It's covered by a protective fog," Dusty explained. "Invisible from above."

The Source was hidden somewhere out in the cornfield. Our task was to find it. Dusty cautioned us to remain vigilant. Obstacles remained in our path—a final set of challenges to prove ourselves worthy Secret Pizza Connoisseurs.

Dusty offered up a piece of advice in the form of a warning: "Beware the rooster. He's the size of a bobcat and as ornery as a wolverine."

Dusty grabbed a milk bucket from a nearby pile and petted Hokey the goat. "Hokey likes to be milked at night," Dusty said. "Don't you, Hokey? Good girl."

Dusty noticed Gloam-pa's compass hanging around my neck. It turned out Dusty had seen the compass before, during a memorable encounter with Gloam-pa back in the 1960s. When Dusty found out Walter Crzytok was my grandfather, he gave me a big bear hug. Dusty offered condolences on Gloam-pa's passing.

"Walter Crzytok! And his buddy with the thick Chicago accent..." Dusty searched his memory.

"Whiskers," I said.

"Yes! Whiskers the Pizza Steward and Walter the Connoisseur. The three of us drank a lot of beer when I visited Chicago. I mean, *a lot* of beer," Dusty laughed.

Gloam-pa was a Connoisseur? Whiskers a Steward?

It made sense, considering the duo's loyalty to Contadino's and the way Gloam-pa instituted Pizza Fridays. But neither Gloam-pa nor Whiskers had any connection to Iowa. Dusty explained that the network of Connoisseurs spread beyond the Hawkeye State. The club was a bare-bones operation compared to The Nexus, but the Connoisseurs maintained modest outposts in every major pizza hub, providing support to family pizza parlors in small towns and city neighborhoods. Dusty praised Gloam-pa's dedication to keeping his affiliation hush-hush. He supposed Gloam-pa left me the compass because I inherited his reverence for pizza.

"Your grandfather gave you his lucky charm for a reason. He saw something special in you, kid," Dusty advised. "Hold on tight to that compass. It'll guide you to The Source."

Dusty plucked a folded orange note from the goat's hindquarters and handed it to Prankster Hank. Dusty waved goodbye and led the goat away to the other side of the barn. Prankster Hank read the note from the goat.

"Shoot," Hank sighed. "Another riddle."

A FAMILIAR DOWNPOUR DOES AWAIT
HE WHO HAILS FROM OUR HOME STATE
USE A BUCKET AS A HEAD SHIELD
TRAVERSE THE TUNDRA TO THE CORNFIELD

Our team peered out the back door at the green cornfield beyond a snow-covered patch of farmland. Prankster Hank pointed up at a cylindrical cloud approaching the barn. It wasn't upright like a tornado, but rather twisting horizontally like a drill bit. It unleashed a storm, only not of raindrops.

"Is that sleet?" I asked.

"Not sleet," Prankster Hank smiled. "It's an Iowa thing."

The cloud took the shape of a corn cob and showered the frozen field with kernels of corn. I was petrified, but Prankster Hank was as cool as a stick of butter, standing still as a silo. He smiled as the giant cloud burst with increased intensity. The cob settled over the barn and bombarded the roof with kernels.

"Where I'm from, it's called 'kerneling,'" Hank said.

"Never heard 'kernel' used as a verb," J.R. Grappler remarked.

Prankster Hank grabbed a milk bucket from the stack and held it out the barn door. A series of pings and clangs rattled our ears as the downpour filled the metal pail. Hank pulled it back into the barn and showed us the bucket full of corn kernels.

"Growing up in Iowa, it was a classic prank. I threw handfuls of corn kernels onto the roof. From inside the house, it sounded like an apocalyptic rainstorm. My dad looked out the window and got all confused because it wasn't raining. It was hilarious!" Prankster Hank giggled.

"We did the same thing in Minnesota with soybeans," Anna chimed in.

Evan gave her a skeptical smirk, and she pushed him playfully.

"I wasn't always a goody-two-shoes," Anna smiled. "I got involved in shenanigans."

"Sure you did," Evan rolled his eyes.

Anna laughed and gave him a kiss.

Prankster Hank emptied the bucket and put it on his head like a helmet.

"Buckets on, everyone," Hank instructed.

Like an army platoon, we did as our colonel ordered. J.R. Grappler accidentally selected a comically small helmet.

"Anyone want to trade buckets?" J.R. laughed.

Prankster Hank took a Carl Lewis stance at the back door.

"Ready?" he called out.

"Ready for what?" I asked.

"Charge!"

Prankster Hank raced out into the corn storm, hopping through the snow like an arctic hare. Kernels pelted him, but the milk pail protected his head. The rest of us watched our friend gallop until he dove headfirst into the cornfield beyond the tundra.

J.R. Grappler ditched his miniature bucket and picked up a large rubber animal feed tub. He gathered Chill Gil and me by his side underneath the upturned tub. On J.R.'s signal, the three of us ran forward in unison, tracing Prankster Hank's path. Anna grabbed Evan's hand, and they ran as a couple, accompanied by Trivia Trixie and Mike Grappler. The buckets and J.R.'s tub provided sufficient protection from the raining kernels. The entire team crossed the snowy grassland without injury. We entered the cornfield.

The first thing I noticed inside the cornfield was the change in climate. It was mild, like the beginning of September. I unzipped my winter coat. The Grappler Twins spotted Prankster Hank sprawled out on the ground with his eyes shut. They rushed over to check on him. Prankster Hank opened his eyes with a big smile.

"That was epic!" he said. "All-time great kerneling!"

29

— • —

MEASURE THE CHEESE

P rankster Hank insisted on staying put to study the corn storm, so we forged on without him. Anna led us through the cornstalks until we came to a clearing. Upon a picnic table sat a bag of white cheese and a simple scale. Trivia Trixie approached the table and found a folded orange note with another riddle:

> AN IOWA STORM HANK LED YOU THROUGH
> NOW THINK ABOUT HIS AIRLINER CLUE
> A MORSEL OVER WILL LEAVE YOU STRANDED
> THIS IS A TASK FOR THE STEADY-HANDED

"If wrestlers know one thing, it's weigh-ins," Mike Grappler stepped forward. "I'll tackle this challenge."

"You?" J.R. Grappler doubted. "I don't think so, dear brother. Back when we played the board game *Operation,* you got shocked trying to remove the funny bone."

"That game is rigged," Mike muttered. "Funny bone isn't even a bone. It's a nickname for the ulnar nerve that runs along the inner elbow."

"There's no more steady hand than Chill Gil," J.R. said. "His resting heart rate is lower than that of a blue whale. A blue whale's heart rate is four to eight beats per minute, for those wondering."

"Good for blue whales," I nodded. "Taking it easy."

Chill Gil took a moment to summon his inner cheesehead, then sauntered up to the picnic table.

"Hank's Airliner clue was Moonlight Graham," Trivia Trixie reminded Gil.

"In the video The Malamute showed us, Raffi Jr. worked nights at Lombardi's in New York," Evan said.

"In other words, he moonlighted," Anna completed the thought. "Alongside George Lombardi, a mozzarella expert."

"Exactly, Hot Lips," Evan smooched her.

As Chill Gil took in all the information being bandied about, he nudged the scale with his forefinger and deemed it accurate.

"Graham is spelled like the cracker," Trixie said.

"Graham crackers," I nodded. "Yum. Let's make s'mores."

"Stay with me, Crust," Trixie snapped her fingers. "A homophone for *G-R-A-H-A-M* is *G-R-A-M*."

"One gram of mozzarella, coming right up," Chill Gil said.

Gil grabbed the bag of cheese and felt its weight in his hands. He reached in and grabbed a pinch of mozzarella. Chill Gil drizzled strands onto the delicate plate of the scale. He paused to check the indicator.

"Ope, a skosh under," Chill Gil said.

Chill Gil adjusted his glasses and sprinkled one shred at a time until it measured precisely one gram. A hidden drawer on the scale popped open. Inside the drawer was one plum tomato, which Gil handed to Evan. Chill Gil inspected the drawer again and found a folded orange note which read:

GIL KNOWS CHEESE
A TRUE PACKERS FAN
TAKE THIS TOMATO
THROW WEST, YOUNG MAN

I consulted Gloam-pa's compass and pointed due west. Evan cocked his arm and chucked the tomato.

Thwack!

The tomato struck a solid, unseen object with a smushy thud. Intrigued, we followed the flying tomato. Trivia Trixie tried to coax Chill Gil into coming along for the next leg of the adventure, but he was fixated on the bag of cheese.

"Remarkable strain of mozzarella," Gil marveled. "Of the highest standard. I can't let this cheese stand alone. I'm sticking here."

"Do your thing, Chester Cheetah," Trivia Trixie said. "Spend some quality time with that cheese."

Trixie double-timed it through the corn to catch up to the rest of us and find out what Evan hit with the tomato.

30

CLASS REUNION

The Malamute trotted onto the Chiron Bridge and peered out over the guardrail. Out on the frozen pond, he spotted Clownfoot and Professor Carson tethered to a toboggan. Clownfoot sat behind the Professor, the laces of his new Reebok Pumps intertwined to keep both hostages restrained. The Malamute climbed over the railing and dropped down onto the ice. As The Malamute tested his footing on the slippery surface, he heard a whistle blow. Pepperoni zoomed out from under the bridge on ice skates to guard the captives aboard the toboggan. Wily Gene emerged from behind a bridge post and blew his whistle again, prompting Pepperoni to press the pumps on Clownfoot's Reeboks. Wily Gene, madman that he was, had rigged the gym shoes. He connected the pumping mechanism to a vat of steaming liquid. A squirt of the slimy substance hit the ice beneath the toboggan each time Pepperoni triggered the pumps.

"That's hot garlic butter!" Wily Gene crowed. "Each pump melts a layer of ice and threatens to plummet your friends into the freezing cold water!"

"Please let Clownfoot and Professor Carson go, Wily," The Malamute pleaded.

"I'll make you a deal, Malamute. Take me to The Source, and I'll release your friends," Wily Gene offered.

"Don't do it, Malamute! We're not worth it!" Clownfoot yelled.

"Speak for yourself, Clownfoot," Professor Carson took exception.

Unwilling to risk the lives of the hostages, The Malamute agreed to escort Wily Gene to The Source. Like a parking valet, Sausage fetched Wily Gene's snowmobile. The Malamute saddled up behind Wily Gene, who climbed into the driver's seat. The erstwhile suitemates sped off the bridge towards the Patterson Seeds property.

31

GRAPPLERS' PEAK

Trivia Trixie burst through the corn into a clearing, where she narrowly avoided bumping directly into J.R. Grappler's backside. J.R. froze in place when he saw the object Evan hit with the tomato: a twelve-foot tall mini-volcano. There was a reason the rock formation gave J.R. a jolt. It was the exact size and shape of a model volcano he once built for a high school science fair project gone terribly wrong.

J.R. Grappler entered the interscholastic competition back in his Hammond, Indiana days. He wanted to design an advanced model volcano that bucked convention. J.R. engineered an electric charge that would give the eruption extra zing. Mike helped him transport the model to the competition in three sections and assemble the seismic mountain on site. When it was showtime, J.R.'s eruption failed. He pressed the button repeatedly, but the lava refused to flow. Frustrated, J.R. descended down into the crater to diagnose the issue. He found a loose wire and made a hasty connection. The volcano transformed into a Super Soaker, dousing onlookers with artificial lava. The principal, the superintendent, and the school's venerable Earth Science teacher were all drenched by the crimson tide. Thankfully, Mike had convinced J.R. to use room-temperature lava, preventing any injuries. Nevertheless, the incident scarred J.R. Grappler's scientific reputation around Hammond.

***

February 8, 1997, Ten O'Clock At Night. Two Hours Until National Pizza Day

J.R. Grappler hung his head after he divulged the details of his high school science fair failure. The academic gaffe haunted him.

"Michael Jordan missed game-winning shots," Evan offered. "You bounced back big time. Look at you now."

"Best lab partner in the world," I confirmed.

A group hug helped J.R. feel better. The relief didn't come without friendly ridicule from his twin brother.

"Hey, J.R.! Was the science fair more embarrassing than the time your singlet ripped open during a meet?" Mike instigated. "Although that was probably worse for the poor wrestling fans who had to see your bare butt."

J.R. playfully shoved his brother to shut him up. Anna found an orange note at the base of the volcano.

TRUE CHEFS VALUE QUALITY OVER EXPEDIENCE
TWINS MUST AGREE ON PROPER INGREDIENTS
THIS TOMATO SAUCE IS THE FINAL TEST
PROVE YOUR TEAM WORTHY OF ITS QUEST

A ledge emerged from the side of the volcano. Upon the ledge sat dozens of mason jars filled with common kitchen ingredients. Mike Grappler climbed to the volcano summit and peered down into the crater. Within the volcano, pureed tomatoes simmered, ready to be transformed into a mouthwatering red sauce. J.R. Grappler shed his winter coat and stepped up to the ingredient shelf.

32

TOBOGGAN TIED

B ack on the hostage toboggan, Clownfoot's stomach was rumbling. He hadn't eaten since lunch in anticipation of the Secret Pizza feast that would occur when Evan and his team inevitably conquered The Source's obstacle course. Professor Carson, bound and tied to the hungry Clownfoot, was experiencing a different biological urgency.

"Mr. Pepperoni? Mr. Sausage? I'd like to officially request a bathroom break," Professor Carson begged. "It was a long ride, and I didn't get a chance to go at the restaurant."

"You stopped at a restaurant?" Clownfoot inquired.

"Yes. We found a charming little mom-and-pop parlor in town. I split a large pizza with Pepperoni and Sausage. Wily Gene ordered his own individual pizza. It was a pleasant meal, all things considered," Professor Carson related.

"Bizarre that Wily Gene would stop for food, but not at his own establishment," Clownfoot noted. "Maybe because he knows he serves crummy pizza."

Beep! Beep! Beep!

An alarm sounded on a pager attached to Sausage's belt. Sausage studied the numerical message on the device and showed it to Pepperoni. The two henchmen skated off into the distance like a pair of Bonnie Blairs, leaving Professor Carson and Clownfoot alone on the frozen pond.

"Think they'll come back for us?" Professor Carson asked.

"Yes. And hopefully they bring food," Clownfoot said. "I'm ravenous. I'd kill for a piece of pizza."

"There are leftovers in the van. Wily Gene didn't finish his individual pizza. He got a doggy bag," Professor Carson said.

Clownfoot craned his neck and spied Wily Gene's van parked near the bridge. Clownfoot needed to eat, but first he needed a plan. He instructed Professor Carson to press the Reebok Pump decompression valves with his nose. The release of air loosened the high tops. Clownfoot wiggled his legs until he was able to slip his feet out of the shoes and untangle the web of laces. Untethered and motivated by hunger, Clownfoot used his enormous feet like seal flippers to propel the toboggan across the ice. It skidded to a stop near Wily Gene's van. Professor Carson hurried to a nearby tree to relieve himself while Clownfoot rummaged through the vehicle in search of leftovers. He found Wily Gene's doggy bag under the seat and replenished his energy reserves with therapeutic pizza.

33

BATTLE ATOP SAUCE MOUNTAIN

J.R. Grappler lobbed jars of olive oil, salt, basil, oregano, and minced garlic up to his brother atop the volcano. Mike balanced on the peak and added each subsequent ingredient. He watched the garlic liquefy and held his hands out to catch the next jar. No toss was forthcoming. Mike peered down at his brother. J.R. picked up a jar of golden honey as he contemplated adding a touch of sweetness to his sauce. Mike balked at the choice.

"Honey? Who are you? Winnie the Pooh? I veto that ingredient, J.R."

"Easy, Mike. I was simply mulling it over as an option. Besides, you don't have veto power."

"The riddle said the twins are supposed to collaborate," Mike said.

"We are collaborating. I'm the head chef, and you're my sous chef."

The smashed tomato Evan had thrown earlier was within Mike's reach. Mike scooped up the goopy mess and hucked it at his brother. The tomato gunk landed on J.R.'s shoulder, staining his treasured "Big Hurt" T-shirt. J.R. glared at his brother, then charged up the mini-mountain. Mike made a move to escape but stumbled and fell headfirst into the crater. He caught himself on the edge with his posterior sticking out the top. J.R.'s anger dissipated instantly. He shifted into lifesaving mode and pulled his brother to safety.

"That was a close one," Mike said. "Thank you, J.R."

"Now who's Winnie the Pooh?" J.R. jabbed. "Stuck in a hole with your butt hanging out."

***

Wily Gene's snowmobile whizzed onto the Patterson Seeds property. Wily Gene circled the barn, and The Malamute directed him toward the fog beyond the snowy field. Wily Gene accelerated into the mist. The vehicle entered the lush cornfield and came to an abrupt halt, sending Wily Gene and The Malamute vaulting over the handlebars and somersaulting to the ground. Wily Gene stood and brushed the dirt off his jeans. He lifted his goggles and stared in wonder at the surreal environment, with its mild temperatures and green plants.

Sitting at the picnic table mere feet away, Prankster Hank and Chill Gil witnessed the snowmobile's crash landing. The carefree duo had been snacking on mozzarella cheese and shooting the breeze.

"You good, Malamute?" Chill Gil inquired.

The Malamute rose to his feet and assured them he was no worse for wear, despite Wily Gene's reckless driving.

"Whoa, you're Wily Gene?" Prankster Hank inquired. "Of Wily Gene's Pizza Canteen?"

Wily Gene bowed. The fame and recognition delighted him.

"Your pizza is nasty, dude," Chill Gil said. "Three bucks I'll never get back."

Wily Gene put his goggles back on and pointed his finger at Chill Gil.

"I guarantee you'll buy my pizza again. In time, your taste memory will fade. You'll see an advertisement for Wily Gene's Pizza Canteen with my shockingly low prices. You'll say to yourself: '*Maybe it wasn't as bad as I remember. Besides, it's only three dollars, and it looks good on television.*'"

"Only to be disappointed when your grody pizza shows up," Prankster Hank said.

Wily Gene pointed his finger at Prankster Hank.

"Perhaps. But once again you've become my customer. Then the cycle re-peats. Eventually, your palate adjusts, and you start to crave Wily Gene's Pizza Canteen."

"Does that really happen?" Prankster Hank wondered.

"Silence!" Wily Gene shouted. "Tell me, what is this place?"

Chill Gil and Prankster Hank stifled a giggle. Gil raised his hand for clarification.

"Do you want us to be silent, or do you want us to tell you what this place is? Mixed messages, Wily Gene."

Prankster Hank and Chill Gil broke into full laughter. The Malamute smirked, too, but provided the answer.

"The edge of the rainbow, Wily Gene. Inside The Source boundaries."

Wily Gene touched a cornstalk to make sure it was real.

"I held up my end of the bargain," The Malamute said. "Now let me go rescue Clownfoot and Professor Carson."

"Not until Secret Pizza's supernatural formula is in my hands," Wily Gene refused.

From the pocket of his wild jeans, Wily Gene produced a cup of Wily Gene's Famous Dippin' Sauce. He approached the picnic table and offered the cup to Prankster Hank and Chill Gil.

"As a gesture of goodwill to a pair of recent customers, I present you with a cup of Wily Gene's Famous Dippin' Sauce," he said. "Go ahead and give it a try."

Wily Gene ripped open the tiny condiment cup and aimed it at Hank and Gil. Once opened, the sauce placed a spell on unsuspecting college students like Prankster Hank and Chill Gil. They were helpless against its powers. They dunked chunks of cheese in Wily Gene's Famous Dippin' Sauce. Moments after consuming the cursed condiment, Hank and Gil fell unconscious with their heads down on the table.

**

After several minutes of deliberation, the Grappler Twins agreed on a final ingredient for their tomato sauce. Mike Grappler added sugar to the mix. The volcano burped and rumbled. A nozzle emerged from the side of the mountain. Trivia Trixie grabbed an empty mason jar, held it beneath the nozzle, and turned the knob. The Grapplers' sauce flowed from the spigot. Trivia Trixie removed one glove. She dipped a fingertip in the sauce and then licked her finger.

"Not bad. Scrumdiddlyumptious, actually."

Trixie capped the jar and threw it in my direction. As I extended my arms to make the catch, I was tackled from behind by Pepperoni and Sausage. The lackeys had been hiding in the corn and waiting for a moment to cause chaos. The henchmen scooped up the jar of sauce. They seemed pleased with their heist. The lackeys' triumph was short-lived, however. The Grappler Twins wrestled Pepperoni and Sausage to the ground and reclaimed the jar.

"That's our sauce," J.R. said.

Wily Gene appeared from the corn with The Malamute as his hostage. They stepped over Pepperoni and Sausage, who were recovering from the Grappler Twins' takedowns.

"Keep your sauce, Grappler Twins," Wily Gene said. "It's of no use to me."

"Then why have your minions blindside Crust?" J.R. demanded.

Wily Gene shrugged.

"I'm paying Pepperoni and Sausage as hired muscle. I might as well have them injure someone."

Evan and Anna helped me to my feet. J.R. Grappler took one menacing step in Wily Gene's direction. The goggled fiend produced a luminous green pepperoncini pepper and aimed it at The Malamute's eyes.

"Stay back! Or I blind him with fiery pepper squirts!" Wily Gene threatened.

"He's not kidding. That's one spicy pepperoncini!" The Malamute's voice quavered.

Wily Gene and his hostage backed away from the Grappler Twins, circling around the volcano.

"The Malamute enlisted each of you for your pizza acumen," Wily Gene shouted. "But what's in it for you as an individual? Nothing. Not a dime. You're sacrificing your time and energy on behalf of some mythical entity. Who stands to profit? None of you. The Source, if it even exists, doesn't respect Connoisseur recruits. It forces you to submit to silly challenges for its own amusement."

I booed. It was in my nature as a baseball fan to boo the opposition. Wily Gene ignored my jeers and continued his propaganda speech with the pepperoncini still pointed at The Malamute's eyes. Wily Gene addressed Anna directly.

"Nanny Margaret was my protector, my sounding board, and my teacher. When the time came to stand up for Margaret and give her credit for the Clunchie, I sided with my wretched parents instead. The fallout caused irreparable harm. That being said, I'm ready to turn over a new leaf. For that reason, I gifted Margaret's niece, aspiring stargazer Astronomer Anna, her first big discovery. Spotting my satellite will be a boost for your career, Anna. I hope this act of generosity serves as adequate repayment for the manner in which I wronged your family with my past actions."

Anna stared at the massive, curly thicket of hair on Wily Gene's head. Her temper flared, thinking of how he had defrauded her Aunt Peggy.

"You've got some nerve, Wily Gene. I have YOU to thank for my discovery? You launched a spy satellite, and you got busted by the Astronomy Club. End of story. Back home in Eden Prairie, when our wiener dog pooped in the house and I found it, I never thanked him either. But at least Doleman showed genuine remorse."

Anna was correct. Wily Gene had no conscience. He had merely learned to feign human emotions. Wily Gene whipped out a look of contrition, which was a tough sell considering he was actively holding a man hostage.

"My apologies, Astronomer Anna. Due credit to your orbital observation. Let me skip ahead to my point. I want you all to be cornerstones of my organization. Wily Gene's Pizza Canteen has deep pockets. With your guidance, we can fund charitable efforts and do real good. The Connoisseurs have no money for donations and no assets to bestow. Forget this Secret Pizza farce and come live in the real world. Join me."

"Don't even consider it," Evan said. "Wily Gene is a bloodsucker. He'll use you like he used my friend Theo. Then he'll jettison you and move on to his next victim."

Wily Gene attempted to smile.

"You speak in hyperbole, Evan. Theo quit his job at Wily Gene's Pizza Canteen. Yet, I still rewarded him with a generous severance package. Six figures. We parted ways amicably. Theo is much wealthier now than, say, when he was working as your record store stock boy."

Wily Gene looked around the clearing, hoping he had swayed some of us to abandon the Secret Pizza cause and join his ranks instead. I knew my group of friends better than Wily Gene did, in spite of the background information he dug up on each of us. No one wavered.

"Face it, Wily Gene. You'll never turn a Connoisseur," The Malamute said. "We're Iowa Strong."

"Don't be so sure, Malamute. Allow me to introduce the newest member of the Wily Gene's Pizza Canteen team. Please give a warm welcome to Iowa City legend Cheez Louise!"

Cheez Louise bumped past Trivia Trixie as she trucked out of the corn and climbed to the summit of the volcano. Louise carried a microphone with her. Although the mic cord wasn't plugged into a speaker, Louise's voice carried.

"It's great to be here," Cheez Louise bubbled. "It's a privilege to accept the role of Public Relations Director at Wily Gene's Pizza Canteen, home of the huge signing bonus for Cheez Louise. Thank you, Wily Gene, for your generosity!"

"Sellout," Trivia Trixie muttered.

Cheez Louise heard Trixie's under-the-breath comment.

"I see we have a heckler! If it isn't Little Miss Can't Be Wrong. Want to come up here and speak into the microphone?"

The bad blood between Louise and Trixie amused Wily Gene. He decided to throw gas on the fire and incentivize a showdown.

"If Trivia Trixie is somehow able to outwit Cheez Louise onstage, I'll free The Malamute and leave without a peep," Wily Gene said.

"I'm no comedian, but I'll give it a shot," Trixie accepted the challenge.

It was decided that Cheez Louise and Trivia Trixie would each get two minutes on the mic. Whoever earned the most laughs would be the victor. Wily Gene promised to be an impartial judge. Cheez Louise went first and targeted us with observational humor. She singled me out as her two-minute set began.

"Hey Weird Beard, the next soft drink you invent should be called 'Peach Fuzz.'"

I kept a straight face, half out of embarrassment and half in loyalty to Trixie. Wily Gene was in stitches, while my friends remained stoic. Cheez Louise called them out for not laughing.

"C'mon, that's funny. Maybe the wrestlers' ears are too cauliflower-ed to hear me clearly. That's a real condition wrestlers get: cauliflower ears. That's why most people choose normal sports, Grappler Twins. When you go bowling, you don't end up with asparagus fingers."

I accidentally laughed at "asparagus fingers" before I caught myself. Cheez Louise had a good delivery.

No one was safe from Cheez Louise's ridicule.

"Pepperoni and Sausage—if those are their real names—are here tonight. In fact, they drove me here on a three-person snowmobile. I don't know what was more awkward: squeezing onto the motor sled between two hulking flunkeys or the fact that neither of them uttered a single word the entire ride. Hey Silent Bob and Silent Bob, where's Jay?"

I straight up guffawed at the Kevin Smith movie reference but stifled myself when Anna shot me a corrective look. For her finale, Cheez Louise took direct aim at her opponent. First, she dug in on Trivia Trixie's lack of height.

"Anybody here from Kansas? Our resident munchkin, Trivia Trixie, would be happy to show you around."

Second, Cheez Louise made fun of Trixie's clothing.

"Ripped jeans are a sign of desperation. It's a way of saying: '*Please notice me and the damaged clothing I purchased.*'"

Finally, Cheez Louise mocked Trivia Trixie's life choices.

"She's an Art major, ladies and gentlemen. Which means after college, she'll be unemployed."

Wily Gene howled with laughter. Cheez Louise bowed and waved the microphone at Trivia Trixie. Trixie didn't hesitate. She marched straight up the mountain and took the mic from the intimidating comic. Cheez Louise chuckled at the dauntless, diminutive trivia champion. She wouldn't have laughed if she knew Trivia Trixie. Cheez Louise was about to get a glimpse of Trivia Trixie's mettle.

Instead of responding to Louise's insults, Trixie calmly shared her thoughts. "I realized something when I was listening to Louise tell jokes on this stage. I recognized her ability to captivate an audience. I listened to her talk about Crust, the Grapplers, and me. The person I really wanted to hear about was Louise. Louise deflects attention, as I do and as many of us do. Louise's one-liners are entertaining, but I'd bet dollars to tomatoes that Louise's personal stories would provide material deeper and more memorable than Crust's admittedly splotchy beard. I have a similar mindset. I overinvest in modesty. I can't accept a compliment. Why can't I say 'thank you' when a friend tells me I'm good at trivia or an expert at solving riddles? I am Trivia Trixie. I am great at trivia. This is Cheez Louise. She is an exceptional comedian. I can only begin to imagine where our talents might lead us in the future."

Anna was the first to applaud. The Grappler Twins, Evan, and I cheered and clapped too. Cheez Louise wiped a tear from her cheek. Trixie's review was the most constructive career feedback she had ever received. Just like that, the petite trivia genius unlocked the comedian's full potential. Cheez Louise realized the key to maximizing her talent would hinge on self-reflection, sincerity, and vulnerability, thereby creating a lasting connection with an audience that could relate. Cheez Louise turned to Trivia Trixie to thank her but couldn't summon the words. Trixie nodded in acknowledgment before finishing up her commentary.

"A bit of positive attention is good for us. A smidge of self-pride is acceptable as long as we don't turn into megalomaniacs like Wily Gene."

The sudden sentimental shift of the showcase made Wily Gene nauseous. He pushed The Malamute to the ground and charged up the mountain. He ripped the microphone from Trixie's hands. Cheez Louise stepped in to stop her new boss from accosting Trixie. Louise and Wily Gene engaged in a tug-of-war. Louise pulled on the cord while Wily Gene clutched the mic.

"Let go of my microphone!" Cheez Louise demanded.

Wily Gene released his grip, throwing Cheez Louise off-balance. She tumbled backwards down the volcano. The comedian landed with a thud. Trivia Trixie rushed down the mountain to help Cheez Louise to her feet. Wily

Gene instructed his lackeys to apprehend Cheez Louise. Pepperoni and Sausage surrounded her, but Cheez Louise swung her microphone like nunchucks and whacked Pepperoni in the forehead. Concussed, Pepperoni collapsed into Sausage's arms.

"My dad took me to Comic-Con every year when I was growing up," Cheez Louise said. "I dressed up as Michelangelo from Teenage Mutant Ninja Turtles. Practiced nunchucks to give my cosplay authenticity. I'm Cheez Louise, and I'm good at nunchucks and cosplay."

Cheez Louise winked at Trivia Trixie. Then she pointed her finger at Wily Gene.

"Consider this my resignation from Wily Gene's Pizza Canteen Incorporated," she said.

Cheez Louise saluted The Malamute and vanished into the corn. Wily Gene commanded Pepperoni and Sausage to follow the escaping employee. Sausage was tending to Pepperoni's head trauma, but he obeyed the boss' order. Sausage led a wobbly Pepperoni into the corn to chase down Cheez Louise.

Wily Gene peered down into the crater at the bubbling red sauce. He noticed the empty jar of sugar near the edge.

"I also prefer a hint of sweetness in my sauce," Wily Gene said. "On the way here, we stopped at a mom-and-pop pizza parlor. They were quite accommodating. Special orders are part of customer service. Right, Evan? I asked them to blend pineapples into my sauce. Family pizzerias will do anything if you ask nicely. Unfortunately, my eyes were bigger than my stomach. I couldn't finish my meal, so I took most of the pineapple-sauce pizza to go. Left the doggy bag in the van. It's parked over by the Chiron Bridge."

"Did you say 'pineapple'?" The Malamute felt a shiver go up his spine.

Wily Gene uncorked a sinister laugh that gave me the willies.

"Yes, pineapple!" Wily Gene chuckled. "My pizza is there for the taking, sitting unattended in my unlocked vehicle. Clownfoot would never steal my leftovers, would he?"

"You monster! You know Clownfoot is allergic to pineapples!" The Malamute screamed.

Anna tossed her Jeep keys to The Malamute so he could drive over to the bridge and warn Clownfoot. Pre-med student Mike Grappler accompanied him in case Clownfoot had ingested the allergen.

"Think your brother can wrestle leftover pizza away from Clownfoot, J.R.?" Wily Gene taunted.

J.R. Grappler regarded Wily Gene as unworthy of a verbal response.

"Don't you dare ignore me!" Wily Gene insisted.

J.R. turned and faced Wily Gene, who remained atop the volcano.

"I did the opposite of ignoring you, Wily Gene. I studied you," J.R. said. "When Crust and I got cornered by The Nexus, Lionel Dwellings made it clear that his organization wasn't the 'green-eyed adversary' Clownfoot cited in the *Connoisseurs' Compendium*—the foe who sought to annex Secret Pizza for profit. My curiosity led me to do a Yahoo search on pizza franchises. I read about the rapid expansion of Wily Gene's Pizza Canteen throughout the Midwest. The founder of the franchise, Eugene Clunch, dropped out of University of Iowa in 1993. I returned to The Nexus office space, where Lionel Dwellings confirmed your vendetta against the Connoisseurs."

Wily Gene scoffed at the mention of The Nexus.

"The Nexus! A robotic conglomerate too big for its own good. Its policies and practices are tragically out of date. The pizza division of The Nexus is sluggish. Its unable to keep pace with new-school operations like Wily Gene's Pizza Canteen."

J.R. Grappler paced back and forth like an attorney about to prove his case.

"Wily Gene is right about The Nexus. It lacks the dexterity for the modern marketplace. A giant can't be nimble. The corporation covers so many bases, from pizza to tacos. The Nexus even has a pet food division. Isn't that right, Wily Gene?"

Wily Gene's upper lip quivered. J.R. Grappler went ahead and answered the rhetorical question.

"Wily Gene pitched Pup Pops to The Nexus a few years ago. His idea was rejected. The Nexus wasn't convinced there was a market for dog popsicles."

"Big whoop," Wily Gene brushed it off. "One failed idea. Word has it you're no stranger to colossal failure, Mr. Science Fair."

J.R. Grappler grinned at Wily Gene's swipe. He produced a piece of paper from the pocket of his blue jeans.

"I stopped by the chemistry lab earlier today to create a formula," J.R. announced. "I combined meat flavoring with other natural ingredients, poured the liquid mix in an ice tray, and popped the tray in the freezer. I have here a copy of a provisional patent claim made by Jeffrey Richard Grappler and Carroll Crzytok for exclusive rights to market Doggy Gloam Pops. The original form is in the mail. Doggy Gloam Pops will soon be available for purchase at Kittle's Pet Shop in downtown Iowa City."

J.R. turned to me.

"Pretty exciting development, eh Crust?"

I smiled in admiration of my lab partner's ingenuity. Wily Gene stomped his feet with rage.

"That's my invention!"

"Doesn't feel good to have your idea stolen, does it?" Anna lectured.

"Snooze you lose, Wily Gene," J.R. smiled.

"How about *you* take a snooze, J.R.?" Wily Gene cried.

He cast a weaponized cup of Wily Gene's Famous Dippin' Sauce to the ground in front of us. The cup glowed and ignited like a Roman candle, shooting buttery sauce in all directions.

"Wily Gene's Famous Dippin' Sauce! One drop will knock you out cold," Wily Gene laughed.

J.R. Grappler threw himself on top of the Dippin' Sauce, sparing us any danger from the liquid spray, but rendering him unconscious.

"Run, Crust!" Anna shouted.

I followed Trixie, Evan, and Anna through the corn until we happened upon a chicken coop. Inside the coop, we climbed a ladder to the second level and hid with the hens. Wily Gene trailed us at a leisurely pace and lingered outside the coop.

"I know you're in the chicken coop, burgeoning Connoisseurs!" he called out. "And I have one more offer. This one is for Evan the Pizza Steward."

We remained silent. Wily Gene leaned against the coop and continued his one-man conversation.

"Wily Gene's Pizza Canteen Incorporated has entered an acquisitional phase. In fact, my company recently purchased a controlling stake in the Phantom Wonderstore. Here's my proposal, Evan: Hand over the secret behind Secret Pizza, and I'll shut down the Wonderstore across the street from Fromager Records. Not only that, I'll prevent any future Wonderstores from opening within twenty-five miles of Naperville."

"I don't even know the secret!" Evan shouted. "We didn't get that far."

Wily Gene, still leaning against the coop casually, cast doubt on Evan's claim.

"You're the apple of The Malamute's eye, Evan—the future of Secret Pizza. The answer is in your head somewhere. Close your eyes and concentrate."

Evan looked at me. I tried to come up with something inspirational to say. Instead, I said, "I lost my compass."

"Gloam-pa's compass?" Evan searched the vicinity.

"Is that it?" Trixie pointed at a nearby nest.

Gloam-pa's compass was resting next to a sleepy hen.

"I'll sweeten the deal, Evan," Wily Gene continued. "I'll sign over the Naperville Wonderstore property to your parents. Fromager Records can expand."

Anna told Evan she'd support him no matter what he decided. I seconded the notion, as Trixie helped me re-secure the compass around my neck.

"My intuition tells me Wily Gene is too inherently dishonest to take him at his word. If you make a deal, be sure to get it in writing," Trixie warned.

Evan's mind was already made up.

"When I made that phone call in Blandville, it wasn't to request a tow truck. I called Theo and apologized for being a steamroller friend. Theo forgave me."

A stray tear trickled down Evan's face. Anna pulled him close and kissed his cheek.

"The record store had a good run," Evan said. "My family would rather see me stay true to my friends and values than barter with the likes of Wily Gene."

"We should throw eggs at him," I suggested, half-kidding.

"Funny you should say that, Crust," Evan smiled. "Theo mentioned that birds dislike Wily Gene. Like, seriously hate him. Wily Gene got pooped on by seventeen different birds during the one year that Theo worked for him. That's beyond a coincidence."

Anna spotted the enormous rooster Dusty had warned us about. The big bird was sleeping soundly on the ground floor of the coop.

"Betcha the rooster would disapprove of Wily Gene stealing his hens' eggs," Anna winked. "Cock-a-doodle-doo."

Anna's plan was to drop eggs into Wily Gene's frizzy hair. It would be easy enough, since Wily Gene was leaning against the coop wall directly below us. Making the eggs stick was the only issue. Luckily, Evan remembered the poster putty in his coat pocket. Trixie helped me sneak two eggs from under the snoozing hen. Anna smeared the sticky, green goop on the eggs and dropped them through a hole in the wire. Wily Gene's natural perm was so puffy, the eggs plopped in and stuck like cherries into whipped cream. Wily Gene didn't feel a thing.

On Anna's signal, I jostled the mother hen. The mama bird squawked and searched frantically for her eggs. Trixie nudged our feathered friend gently over toward the opening in the coop wire, where the hen caught sight of her eggs in Wily Gene's headnest. The commotion roused the rooster, who hopped into action. The rooster busted out the coop door and turned the corner toward Wily Gene. The pizza magnate was unaware the wattled beast was bearing down on him until a talon to the thigh pierced his wild jeans and drew blood. Wily Gene shrieked and tried to run, but his gouged leg gave out and he collapsed to the ground. The rooster raked at his head, tearing at Wily Gene's scalp and ripping out chunks of frizz. The sticky eggs remained tangled in his hair. Wily Gene scrambled to his feet and fled into the cornfield. The rooster pursued, clawing at the egg thief. Wily Gene's screams echoed throughout the farm as my friends and I stepped out of the coop.

The rooster soon returned. He swaggered past us, drenched in Wily Gene's blood, and looked quite proud of protecting his brood. The magnificent bird merely glanced in our direction, yet I was compelled to nod in respect.

"He's gotta be up early tomorrow," I said.

Trixie pointed at my chest. Gloam-pa's compass shimmered. The magnetic needle spun in circles, then came to a dead stop. I held the compass aloft like a drum major's baton and followed the needle into the corn. Evan, Anna, and Trixie marched behind me, as Gloam-pa's compass showed us the way.

34

MUSH GOES THE MALAMUTE

The Malamute and Mike Grappler arrived at the Chiron Bridge. They found Professor Carson tending to Clownfoot, who was dizzy and struggling to catch his breath. Mike examined Clownfoot's swollen jowls and recommended getting him to a hospital posthaste.

Mike strapped Clownfoot to the toboggan like a makeshift gurney. He, Professor Carson, and The Malamute lifted Clownfoot into the back of the Wily Gene's Pizza Canteen van. The Malamute summoned his Alaskan delivery driver skills to conquer the snowy roads on the way to the closest hospital in Cedar Rapids.

"Hang in there, buddy," The Malamute said, glancing at the rearview mirror.

"He's losing consciousness!" Mike shouted.

The Malamute kept talking in order to keep Clownfoot alert.

"By the way, you were right all along, Clownfoot. Wily Gene's mansion is on Lake Winnibigoshish. I asked him during our snowmobile ride."

The severe allergic reaction constricted Clownfoot's windpipe, but Professor Carson could tell he was trying to communicate something. The Professor leaned his ear close to Clownfoot's mouth. Clownfoot wheezed out a few words before he lost consciousness again.

"What did he say?" The Malamute asked.

"Lake Winnibigoshish," Professor Carson relayed the message. "Clownfoot says, 'Told you so.'"

The Malamute smiled and pressed down on the accelerator. Mike Grappler performed CPR while Professor Carson measured Clownfoot's pulse. The van arrived at Livingston Hospital, where nurses rushed Clownfoot to the emergency room.

35

— ◦ —

THE SOURCE REVEALED

**February 9, 1997, One Minute Past Midnight.
National Pizza Day**

Back at the Patterson Seeds farm, Gloam-pa's compass led us to a tiny wooden shack at the center of the cornfield. Anna knocked, and the door slowly creaked open. We entered and found ourselves in a vintage kitchen. Standing with his back to us, a pizza chef dusted his work surface with cornmeal and reached for a dough ball.

"Raffi Jr.?" Evan whispered in wonder.

"But he'd be over one hundred years old," Trixie said.

The chef, who seemed to be of a bygone era, turned to us and waved hello.

"Hi," I waved back.

"Your pizza will be ready in twenty-five minutes," the chef said in an accent that blended Italian and Midwestern.

The chef returned to stretching the dough. Anna was mindful of allowing the chef his space and recommended we wait outside.

"Drives my dad bonkers when folks hang over his shoulder at the grill," Anna said.

The wait allowed us time to wake J.R., Hank, and Gil from Wily Gene's Famous Dippin' Sauce-induced slumbers. One sip of Gloam Pop, with its exorbitant caffeine content, revitalized our friends. Alert and energized, Prankster Hank endorsed Gloam Pop as capable of rousing Rip Van Winkle.

We returned to the tiny shack, where Anna invited the "sleepyheads" to "take a gander" at Raffi Jr.'s kitchen. The timing was impeccable, as our order was ready for pickup. Evan thanked Raffi Jr., who winked and thanked us in return.

The door of the shack closed behind us, and a flock of starlings nosedived out of the mist. We backed away as the circling birds enveloped the shack, obscuring it from view. A minute later the cyclone of starlings ascended back up into the thick fog. The shack had disappeared.

Evan carried the pizza through the cornfield. Anna noticed a trail of blood that led us to conclude Wily Gene was helped to his snowmobile by Pepperoni and Sausage. Chill Gil reported hearing snowmobiles whizzing away in the distance.

Evan led us back to the picnic table, where we could sit and eat together. I moaned with delight upon my first taste of the sensational pizza. My audible enjoyment elicited giggles around the table.

"Secret Pizza from The Source. Nothing better," I said.

The pizza feast commenced. I was so busy stuffing my face, it took me a few minutes to notice that Evan wasn't eating. He claimed he wasn't hungry. Anna asked if he was feeling alright.

"Don't want to use my Steward powers and send everyone off into dreamland. After all, I've got a million things to do. Not only am I worried about Clownfoot, I've got to get my car towed out of Blandville..."

Anna touched his arm and urged him to savor the once-in-a-lifetime moment.

"Finish what you started here," she advised.

Evan looked around the table. Chill Gil debated cheese-to-sauce ratio with J. R. Grappler. Trivia Trixie conspired with me to attach a Post-it note to Prankster Hank's back. Evan felt the warmth and joy of friends around him. He let go of his worries and took a bite of Raffi Jr.'s pizza. It sent us on a trip, albeit with a twist. Our group all traveled together at Raffi Jr.'s side, from Italy to New York City, through the United States, and finally to Iowa, where Raffi Jr. found his everlasting home. An instant later we were back at the picnic table, each one of us now wholly appreciating the significance of Secret Pizza. We understood the struggle and the journey required to make pizza an institution. Our goal was suddenly clear and simple: protect and support neighborhood pizzerias. We had graduated into full-fledged Connoisseurs.

36

— . —

Epilogue

M ike Grappler drove Anna's Jeep back to the Patterson Seeds property
and updated us on Clownfoot's medical condition. We piled into the
SUVs and hurried to Livingston Hospital.

We arrived to find The Malamute on an outdoor bench, clutching Clownfoot's shark tooth pendant between his palms. He stared past us, off into the
dark parking lot.

"He's...gone," The Malamute uttered.

Professor Carson walked out through the revolving door. He confirmed the
devastating news.

"Doctors said he put up a heckuva fight," Professor Carson managed, battling back tears.

***

Clownfoot's actual funeral took place on Maui, but his family honored our
request to hold a separate remembrance in Iowa City the following week. The
Connoisseurs of Iowa City were all present. Professor Carson and Cheez Louise
also attended. Clownfoot's Film class contemporaries paid their respects as well.

The Malamute stood and said a few words about living with Clownfoot,
their tendency to debate topics both trivial and monumental, and the loyalty that Clownfoot exhibited throughout their friendship. I cried during The
Malamute's eulogy. The recessional hymn was a somber Tupac ballad.

One-Eyed Jakes hosted a reception following the service. Iowa City parlors donated dozens of pizzas. A pair of Clownfoot's Reebok Pumps sat on display next to a portrait I sketched. The gym shoes inspired me to approach the DJ booth and request "Pump Up The Jam" in Clownfoot's memory. The DJ nodded and began a search for the album. A guy standing near the speakers praised my song request.

"Title track of Technotronic's 1989 debut album," he said. "Good choice."

"It's also on *Jock Jams: Volume 1*," I responded.

The stranger shook my hand.

"You must be Crust. Evan mentioned you."

Evan spotted us conversing and rushed over to hug the stranger.

"Crust, do you know who this is?" Evan asked. "This is...well, I'll let him introduce himself."

"Theo," the stranger said.

"Theo! Evan speaks highly of you. Pleasure to finally meet the other half of the THREE-O SCALE creative team."

Evan escorted Theo over to meet Anna, who was thrilled to make Theo's acquaintance. After a few minutes of chatting, Anna asked if Theo would drive Evan to Pagliai's to get her an onion pizza. Theo handed Evan his Bulls coat, and the two old friends departed to run the errand. I questioned Anna's need for another onion pizza.

"Pagliai's already delivered plenty of onion pizza," I told her.

"I know, Crust," Anna responded. "Figured Evan and Theo could use a bit of one-on-one time."

Evan and Theo hadn't buddied around in over a year. As a result, they struggled to find a conversational flow as Theo's car started up in the cold. It didn't help that Theo's stereo was on the fritz, so there was no music to melt the ice. Small talk kept the silence at bay.

"How long was the drive here?" Evan asked.

"Three hours. Not too bad," Theo answered.

Evan directed him to Pagliai's. They placed the order at the hostess stand and grabbed a booth while they waited.

"This is where I met Anna. Crust and I were sitting in this exact booth," Evan recalled.

"Anna seems like a cool girl," Theo said.

"She is. Anna's the best."

The awkwardness lingered. Evan started to fear he'd never recapture the natural rapport he had with his oldest friend.

Maybe we've both changed too much.

"You really met Bob Fomptelonski's granddaughter?" Theo asked. "What are the odds that you ran into someone with the last name Fomptelonski?"

"Astronomical," Evan replied.

Theo started whistling the *RBI Baseball* theme music. Evan smiled and whistled along. Soon, they were singing in unison:

> *"Bob Fomp-te-lon-ski*
> *Oh Bob Fomp-te-lon-ski*
> *Oh Bob Fomp-te-lon-ski*
> *Right now..."*

Evan and Theo shared a great laugh—the kind of spontaneous laughter that only happens in the company of a dear friend.

The floodgates of conversation opened up. Evan caught up on Theo's favorite new albums and advised him to check out the Minnesota-based band Anna recommended. When the pizza was ready, Evan opened the box and offered Theo a piece. For a moment, it felt like they were back at Fromager Records.

"Fresh onions, caramelized cheese, nice bite," Theo graded the pizza. "I'd rate it a ninety-one overall."

"Whoa! Highest rating ever! We never cracked the ninety barrier before," Evan said. "Ninety-one means it's the best pizza on record."

The easygoing chatter continued all the way back to One-Eyed Jakes. Theo stopped but didn't put the car in park. It was time for him to head back to Wisconsin.

Theo handed Evan an envelope containing two $50,000 personal checks—one made out to B.J's Pizza and the other to Pizzeria Garza.

"This is your severance money from Wily Gene's Pizza Canteen," Evan realized.

"The way you described Blandville over the phone...I hate to see any town robbed of its local pizza parlors," Theo sighed. "Figured the Connoisseurs could use this money to help revive those establishments."

"Dude, this is a lot of dough," Evan said. "You sure about this?"

"Yep. Starting a new job tomorrow. It pays well," Theo winked.

The crowd at One-Eyed Jakes had dwindled down to only The Malamute, Anna, J.R., Hank, Gil, Trixie, and me. The Malamute was holding court at a circular table. Evan set the onion pizza in front of Anna and grabbed a seat.

"Glad you're back, Evan," The Malamute said. "I was about to reveal the secret ingredient in Secret Pizza."

"It's gotta be olive oil from the blessed olive tree Raffi Jr. carried to America," I guessed.

"Could be the cornmeal," Prankster Hank pointed out. "Why else would Raffi Jr. settle amongst the cornfields of Iowa?"

"The secret is that there is no secret ingredient," Evan said.

"Interesting, Evan," The Malamute responded. "Please explain."

Evan detailed his thought process.

"Wily Gene was never a threat to steal the secret ingredient because even a world-class charlatan can't steal something he can't quantify. Wily Gene uses pizza for profit. He doesn't appreciate what it means to order a hot pizza with your closest friends on a frigid study night or how coworkers bond over pizza and beer after a long day on the job..."

Evan paused and looked at me.

"...or the significance of Pizza Friday for a kid and his beloved grandfather."

I felt a lump in my throat, but I was fresh out of tears to cry at the end of a sad day.

"Let me get this straight: If I order a Secret Pizza at Falbo's, is it simply a regular pizza?" Chill Gil asked.

"Essentially," The Malamute confirmed. "The supernatural element isn't tangible. Secret Pizza derives its energy from the virtues of loyalty, friendship, and devotion. Consider the challenges your team completed and the riddles you solved together. Your friends assisted, each bringing unique skills and knowledge to the equation. Finding The Source is a test of friendship. Evan's natural ability as a Pizza Steward is useless without his band of passionate Connoisseurs, who believe that there are traditions in this world worth preserving."

"Jiminy Christmas! Jumped through all those hoops just to find out the secret ingredient is 'friendship,'" Anna wisecracked.

"Sorta cheesy. But I suppose a pizza quest merits a cheesy ending," Trivia Trixie quipped.

The Malamute shared a wistful memory.

"Our freshman year, when Clownfoot found out there was no actual physical secret ingredient, he was convinced we missed something. He forced us to go through every clue ten times before I finally convinced him Secret Pizza didn't involve psychedelic tomatoes or charmed cheese."

The Malamute sniffled and dried a tear with his napkin. We raised our drinks to Clownfoot, the fallen Chief Connoisseur.

"Hey, J.R., where's Mike?" Chill Gil asked.

J.R. Grappler sighed.

"My brother intended to make it down from Minnesota for the service, but had a change of plans. Mike was offered an internship at the Mayo Clinic, on the condition that he join the Golden Gophers chapter of The Nexus as a Pizza Intrepid. The decision weighed heavily on his conscience. Ultimately, for an aspiring doctor like Mike, the chance to study at the renowned Mayo Clinic was a phenomenal opportunity."

In a day littered with emotions, the surprising news hardly made a ripple. J.R. was disappointed but understood his brother's decision.

"He told me The Nexus hired a new Midwest GM to lead them into the next millennium. Mike didn't mention the guy's name, but word is he's a prodigy."

"His name is Theo," Evan said.

"Your Theo?" Anna gasped.

Evan nodded.

"Your brother is in solid hands," Evan told J.R. "Theo is a good man. He won't steer Mike wrong."

After last call, we loitered in front of One-Eyed Jakes to exchange goodbye hugs. In the spirit of hope for brighter days ahead, Trivia Trixie announced she was using the Spring Break airline tickets she won at Micky's to visit New York City.

"Who gets the second ticket?" Anna inquired.

"Crust," Trixie said. "But let it be known we're only going as friends."

"Of course," I agreed. "Speaking of which, can we stop at the coffee shop where they hang out on *Friends*?"

"Central Perk isn't an actual coffee place, Crust," Trixie broke it to me. "The *Seinfeld* diner is real, though. Plenty of time to map out all the TV tourist attractions."

"Spring Break of my dreams," I smiled.

J.R. Grappler, Prankster Hank, and Chill Gil discussed a ski trip to Breckenridge. Evan scored tickets to the Miami Open pro tennis tournament. He was taking Anna, on the condition that she not run on the court to steal a kiss from Andre Agassi.

"No promises," Anna laughed. "Watch for me on *SportsCenter*."

"I'm flying to Hawaii," The Malamute said. "Clownfoot's cousin invited me for a visit. She assured me the sea breeze keeps the island cool at night."

***

The next night, Evan and I stayed in and watched MTV in our dorm room. *Beavis & Butt-Head* cut to commercial, and the block led off with a brand new ad for Wily Gene's Pizza Canteen. Makeup covered his wounds, but I could tell that Wily Gene was still bruised and battered from the rooster attack. His latest deal offered consumers three large BBQ chicken pizzas for ten bucks.

"Apparently Wily Gene is taking revenge on the poultry population," I commented.

Evan shook his head in disgust at the false advertising. It was a gross misrepresentation of Wily Gene's slimy ingredients.

"Wily Gene is a total budlacker," Evan scoffed. "As Clownfoot would say."

We paused in remembrance of our late friend as Wily Gene preened on-screen. The diabolical menace lurked as an existential threat to every independent pizzeria in the United States. Evan acknowledged that the success of his Stewardship would hinge on continuously outmaneuvering Wily Gene.

Around midnight, Evan mentioned we hadn't eaten since dinnertime.

"Hungry, Crust? Wanna order a pizza?"

I gave my roomie a definitive double thumbs-up.

Evan opened his Trapper Keeper, and we began the search for our next pizza experience.

— ❦ —

Acknowledgments

The author would like to extend special thanks to:

Gifted storyteller and lifelong friend Dan Loftus, for his encouragement as I neared the finish line.

Mentor and advisor Brian Loftus, the first individual I trusted with a written draft. Indebted to Brian for taking a Hawkeye freshman under his wing back in the day.

Brian and Nicki Blattner, who welcomed me to Missoula as an honorary member of the family. I improvised an after-dinner story for Ben and Luke's amusement. An Iowa City pizza adventure began to take shape...

Made in the USA
Monee, IL
13 March 2024

54977317R00121